Destiny's Bond

Book One of the Veldar Chronicles

Everlee Lake

Unbound Publishers LLC

Contents

Chapter One

♥

Hope Rosedale, a beautiful high Elf, ran down the hallway from her bedroom holding her nightgown high to her knees. She did not want to wear a corset and by Gods, she wouldn't. She raced down the stairs and into the throne room, forgetting her state of dress. Her father, the king, stood from his black marble throne and yelled, "Hope! Back to your room. Such a disgrace. Go!" A group of diplomats turned in her direction and ogled the barely grown Elven princess.

Hope's smile faded. Salty tears stung her eyes. She ran back the way she came. Rose, her maid, stood at the top of the stairway and held her arms out.

"Don't let it get to you, sweetling," Rose said. Hope buried her head into Rose's shoulder and the pair walked back to Hope's room to get her dressed. Rose had been with the family for as long as Hope could remember. She was an older Elf, with black hair and green eyes. She always kept her hair up in a tight bun. Rose was tiny and looked child-sized compared to Hope. She loved Hope like her own daughter, and Hope loved her like a second mother, since Tobias, her father, had prevented Hope and her birth mother from meeting.

"Oh, why do I have to wear these stuffy things, Rose?"

Rose ignored her question. The laces strained around Hope's middle and Hope squeaked in surprise.

"Your father wants you to find a good match after this Midsummer festival, perhaps at the festival, your ladyship."

"Perhaps. It'd be great if father wasn't pushing certain suitors my way."

"Maybe he knows who is best for you?"

"Let's just concentrate on today. I don't even want to think about it right now. We're going shopping. I'd like to have a good time."

Hope's day gown was cut to show her décolletage, blue to match her eyes with golden threads accenting the bodice. Sapphire slippers adorned her feet. Her pale-colored complexion blended well with the dress. Rose messed with and then combed out and placed a jeweled flower into Hope's corn silk platinum hair that fell in waves to the small of her back. Rose looked her over.

"Perfect. Go now, see your father."

"Yes, Rose. I don't want to." Hope mumbled as she walked away.

Hope softly padded to the throne room and found her father sitting on his throne. Tobias Rosedale, one of the most handsome males in all Veldar stood up towering over her at six foot six, odd for a Half-Elf. Unlike the rest of his family, Tobias was dark-complected and finely chiseled. Thick waves of pitch hair drawn back in a ponytail only helped the look. He had a Nubian nose, full lips, dark piercing eyes, almost black, and rippling muscles up and down his chest, back and arms. He wore a tight-fitting fencing shirt and riding pants with a belt. His method of dress, always impeccable. Gold and jeweled rings glinted as he pressed his hands together.

"Hope, my lovely daughter. It is an honor to see you. You've been granted a special gift this year. The lottery was picked for those now of age and your name came up to be Midsummer Night's Queen. Isn't that wonderful?"

His voice was stern. She knew there would be no getting out of this. No choice on her part. Tobias the Great had spoken.

In her best exuberant voice, Hope answered, "Yes, Papa! That is wonderful. I look forward to it. Although, I don't know what to do. Who can I ask for help?"

"I will bring in last year's Queen to help you in every way that you need. You will be exquisite."

Hope's nerves were on edge. She knew some strange Elf in a mask would be chasing her, but that was about all. The King of Midsummer's mission was to capture and woo the Queen before the short night was over to ensure a good harvest. Hope had twenty days to prepare herself. She was about to become popular. Hope's eyes refocused as she heard her name.

"Hope. Hope? Are you listening to me?" her father demanded.

"Yes, I was just caught up daydreaming about the festival. I apologize."

"Here, take my signet ring. Go get Rose. Go shopping for some resplendent dresses and gowns. Spare no expense. This is your time, daughter."

Hope's eyes brimmed with tears. She blinked several times, then hugged her father suddenly and it made him startle. "Thank you, father."

The princess ran up the stairs to her room looking for Rose. She reached the top of the stairs and screeched as she slid and busted her rear end on the hard marble floor.

"M'lady! Are you hurt?" exclaimed Rose as she rushed to her side.

"Nothing my pride can't handle. We're going shopping!"

"All that fuss over a shopping excursion. And Hope, ladies don't run. They set the pace."

"Well, my circumstances called for a *fast* pace. Get your things. We're going uptown on dad's tab." She showed her the ring.

Rose's eyebrows shot up. "Indeed. You will look quite lovely, and that's what I'm afraid of your ladyship. Can barely keep an eye on you now."

Both women descended the palace stairs of fine black marble interlaced with golden veins. The floor was sparkling, as were the walls. Hope remembered fondly when she and her brothers would run and slide on the floors leaving streaks to make the housekeepers angry. Tapestries of black and gold thread with the country's symbol, the golden rose, hung on each wall in grandiose fashion.

The two women boarded the fine carriage. "Fairfax Furs, please!" Hope called. As they rode through town Hope peeked out the window and spied many attractive noblemen. Oh, how she hoped some of them would be at the festival.

"Starting expensive are we, Milady?" Hope grinned at her and nodded and continued staring out the window. "Whatever are you staring at like that?"

"Life. People. I feel like I'm caged in up there sometimes. I'm starting to look forward to being Midsummer Queen."

They walked throughout the mall area and Humans, Elves, and even one brave Dwarf offered sweets, flowers, and tokens of their adoration to Hope. She was so tickled that she giggled and blushed at each one. She gave the Dwarf a big kiss on the nose. That flustered him to no end, and he lost all his nerve and stumbled off mumbling nonsense to himself. On the last stop at the jeweler, a very tall Half-Elf swooped a hello in front of Hope while Rose had her attention elsewhere.

"Hi Milady. I'm Typhon of St. James." He leaned in over her hand but slipped her glove off quickly in the process and the heat between their skin mingled and Hope gasped. Typhon's hand slid to the small of her back, and he pulled her in, the sheer electricity engulfed them. He couldn't stop himself. He gently slanted his mouth over hers and pulled her off in the alley. Hope's lips fell open in another gasp, and he delved his tongue in. Hope trembled from the new feelings that overwhelmed her body.

Under heavy lids, she looked into his eyes. When their eyes met, the magic began its work. He heard her thoughts. She felt his feelings. Her eyes widened, then she relaxed and surrendered to his embrace. He kissed her deeply. He felt, saw, heard, and sensed her pleasure. *Who was this woman?* She cried out as he trailed hot kisses down her throat.

Rose heard Hope's cry and worried. She ran toward the noise. "For the sake of the holy!" Rose's voice raised octaves from behind the pair. Rose started beating Typhon with her bag. "Just what do you think you're doing with her Ladyship? Hands off!"

The magic and whoosh of high emotion shattered like glass. Typhon's face fell to stone, and he mouthed *her Ladyship*. "Hope, er rather, Princess Hope?" Typhon asked the beauty in his arms. Hope nodded silently.

"Yes, you big oaf. Take your scandalous hands off her before I knock you on your arse!" Rose warned and put space between the two of them with her body.

"He didn't do anything I didn't allow. I hope to see you at the Midsummer Night's Ball." Hope said.

"Wouldn't miss it." With a flourish of his cloak, he bowed low. "Save me at least two dances, your Ladyship."

Rose snarled and went after him again with her bag. "Not if I have anything to say about you won't! Rascal!"

"Rose, it's okay. We'll be in public at the ball. What could happen?"

"Might I point out that you were in public today? You better hope nobody was watching or else you're ruined."

"Ha! It'd be nice to be independent."

"*Get* in that carriage."

Nothing could break Hope's joy. She'd never felt like that before. That Half-Elf was so perfect.

Rose looked at Hope with slits for eyes.

"We didn't. I swear. I mean he took some liberties, but he did not do anything like *that*."

"Well, there's something strange about you. Some sort of magic. Was he a caster?"

"Not that I'm aware of. I don't know," she looked at her arms. They had a slight white glow to them, "this makes no sense."

Rose started the incantation to the familiar spell Dispel and it failed to dissipate the magic on Hope's body. Rose tried several times, and it failed each time. "That Half-Elf is a strong caster. Stronger than I. This means trouble, Hope. Stay away from him. I mean it. When you get home run your hind end up to the bath immediately."

While Hope was bathing, Rose went to see Tobias in his study. "Your daughter was out today, but I caught her nearly compromised by one Typhon St. James, the crown prince of that same country. I think he's taken with her. I doubt that's the last we've seen of him. What's worse, they were bonding. Something I haven't seen in centuries. Your child has that ability, so we had better be extra careful now with her. Anyone finds out and casters of all types will be after her."

"Thank you, Rose. I must plan my next move. Continue to keep an eye on my daughter. I will raise your pay."

Chapter Two

♥

Typhon watched the carriage pull away. He stood and shook his head as he tried to understand what had just happened. That was the most perfect lady he had ever laid eyes on. *We were so close to...what?* He had heard her voice in his head and felt her passion as his own. He had to go see his mother, Ilyanna, the Enchantress of St. James. Maybe she would know of this.

Typhon left for his home. The reason he had come to Rosedale was long forgotten. This was much too important. He rode all night and half the morning to get to the borderlands. He stopped to let his horse drink at the river dividing Rosedale and St. James. Behind him, he heard a sing-song voice.

"Hello."

He turned. He saw a gorgeous barely dressed nymph standing before him. His eyes widened as he took in her beauty. "Hello."

"I'm lonely. Keep me company. I do so long for the touch of a man." She ran her delicate hand up his chest and kissed him gently on the lips.

Typhon felt drunk. *Would it be a relief to lie with the nymph and just get it over with?* His mind flickered back to Hope's beautiful, flushed face and half-opened lids. His head swam.

The nymph gently pressed him down into the grass. She climbed atop him. A helpless gasp escaped Typhon's mouth. He kept thinking about Hope. The nymph's face changed to Hope's and Typhon's riding pants grew tight.

"Where did you learn to do that, Hope?"

"I have many secrets." she cooed back.

The magical glow started to surround his body. She leaned down to kiss him but then jumped back.

"Hope?"

The nymph backed away. "Don't touch me! You are the Star Seed's mate."

"What?"

The nymph ran back into the woods and disappeared before Typhon could get any more information out of her. He'd had enough interruptions. He sped across the valley until his home city came into view and didn't stop until he'd reached the castle proper. He handed his steed off to a guard and went directly to find his mother. His ex-lover was visiting court. She stepped out of a darkened hallway in front of him.

"Hello, Typhon." She placed a hand on his chest. Her long, silky, raven hair fell about her. Her dress was so low-cut Typhon's eyes were drawn toward the slit in her bodice that revealed her navel. She was gorgeous, and she knew it.

"I'm needing to see my mother at the moment," he stepped back from her hand, "I'll catch up with you later, Mawyn."

She pouted. Her green eyes sparkled when they met his. "Promise?"

Typhon sighed and ran a hand through his hair, "Yes."

Ilyanna St. James was a delicate but strong Elven woman of 2285 years. She loved her son and husband more than life itself. Her long golden hair and gray eyes had passed to her son. She was tan, unlike most Elves. She absolutely loved the sunshine. She had been reading some ancient tome in the dusty old library when her son barged in.

"Mother, I need your help."

"Whatever is the matter, son. You're glowing with magic. Come, sit, tell me what happened. Are you sick, poisoned, wounded?"

"No, just really confused." Typhon relayed the entire story including the nymph to his mother hoping she'd understand.

"First of all, why in Veldar did you almost compromise the Crown Princess of Rosedale?"

"I didn't know it was her."

She arched her brow. "Second, this magic is ancient. It's rare and something not to be taken lightly. You are bonding with Princess Hope. It's an Elven bond. As for the Star Seed, that's dangerous. I've only heard of one Star Seed in all my years. She was hunted down and repeatedly kidnapped by men of great power. Star Seeds can give birth to immortals. What's worse is they are inherently magical. You'd better find Hope. Handfast her and bring her home so we can protect her here. Keep this to yourself. You do not want anyone to find out. Not even Hope's family. They are not all they seem. Trust me."

The gravity of the situation settled on Typhon's shoulders. "I want my father's blessing."

"And you shall have it."

Typhon headed to prepare for his journey to Rosedale capital. He knew the Ball was tomorrow. He would do the proper thing and ask for her hand. While he relaxed in his bath, Mawyn barged into his room.

"Mawyn! Get out. I'm bathing."

She sauntered over to him. She smiled wickedly. Her dress pooled at her feet. Mawyn got into the water with him. She walked straight up to him and placed a kiss on his lips.

"No, Ma..." he murmured. Her tongue slid into his mouth. Their tongues met and he felt her tongue piercing. He winced. It took everything he had but he slid his hands carefully to her sides and gently pushed her away. Mawyn's eyes met his. She ran her hands down his rippled arms. He trembled.

"My Prince?" She asked, confused.

Oh gods, if she only knew how hard this is. I want to bed her right now. His thoughts swam. Memories of their time together sped through his mind.

"You must go. I can't. Things aren't the same anymore."

"I...see," she climbed out of the bath. He watched her every movement as she left.

He was so aroused. He didn't know what to do. Typhon laid back and tried to clear his head. He drifted off to sleep. A noise in the other room woke him. He went out to investigate. A shock when he turned the corner and came to face Lavinia, Mawyn's little sister.

"What in nine hells are you doing here?"

Her gaze was fixed on his groin. She blushed. "I, uh, was looking for Mawyn."

"Lavinia, my eyes are up here."

"I know it's just so *huge*. I never thought one could be so big."

Typhon laughed. "I am flattered, but really you'll be ruined if you're found in my room alone."

She stared at his groin, her eyes flicked to his rippled chest, strong arms and legs. She started to bite her lip. Typhon watched her reaction curiously. Her chest heaved.

"Lavinia, sweety, you must go. I'm concerned about your reputation, but I'm not going to carry you out. Lavinia?"

"Right. I need to go." She gave her head a shake. "Rules, propriety. All that." She mumbled as she backed out the door and into someone. Lavinia's breath stopped in a huff.

"Well, what would Lady Lavinia be doing in Prince Typhon's bed-chamber?" Lavinia turned and faced the foulest gossip of the court.

"Uh, I was looking for my sister, Lady Silvermoon."

"Really," she purred, "well that's unfortunate for you to be found sneaking out of a man's bedchambers."

Lavinia's eyes widened, "I didn't do anything. He was a gentleman. What are you going to do?"

"Inform the proper people, of course, Lady Lavinia. It's only the right thing." Lady Silvermoon turned on Lavinia and walked off with a sarcastic laugh.

Lavinia felt sick. She tapped on the Prince's door. He opened the door, still stark naked. When he saw her face, he yanked her inside his bedchamber.

"What happened, Lavinia?"

"Lady Silvermoon. I shut the door and turned around and there she was. I'm ruined."

Typhon took a deep breath. He was furious. Tomorrow, he was supposed to have asked for Hope's hand, now he had to figure out what to do with a young human teenager that was now ruined by her curiosity.

She looked up at him. Lavinia was aware of his mood shift. She felt emotions easily. Her body tensed. Lavinia expected his anger.

He turned away from her. She watched him as he stood, his shoulders heaved. Lavinia reached out and ran her fingers down his back. She didn't know what to do. Out of fear and a need to comfort him, she lightly touched his arm.

"My Lord?"

In one quick motion, he turned back to face her. Her shock was evident. She stepped back and lost her footing. He caught her. Typhon pulled her close. Her breath caught. His hand grasped her hair clips and loosed her long black hair with a silver streak from her temple. She gasped. His strong hand lifted her chin up. His eyes were a thunderstorm.

"I'm going to kiss you now, Lavinia."

Chapter Three

♥

"The ultra-famous Rosedale Midsummer Ball is tonight, and I can't wait," Hope exclaimed to herself aloud. She began dressing in a shift and then a pure white diamond-encrusted bodice dress that went to the floor. She thought about Typhon, blushed a little, and put on new sexier intimate underclothes that no one knew about.

Outside the castle, Typhon was dressed as the Crown Prince he was. Typhon was ready to present himself to King Rosedale and ask for Hope's hand. He had his own father's blessing. He was ready. He was led into the castle with many others including Donovan Darkblades.

Donovan Darkblades was an Elf that stood 5'2" tall and had black sleek hair that was tousled on his head. His eyes were dark brown, almost black. Wide awake, he looked as if he were regal and knew it. Like a walking ego. He wore all black and was impeccable in his clothing taste. He stood in the corner and watched everyone with his arms crossed over his chest. His eyes scanned the crowd as he waited.

The Royal family was announced one by one. Donovan and Typhon both perked up at the sound of Hope's name. Flanked by a half dozen guards on each side, the Royal family took their places on the dais, with Tobias on the throne. Shouts of "Long live the King!" went up in the audience everywhere when he sat down. A line formed of those wishing to offer their gratitude and thanks to the king. Typhon got in line for a different reason. When Typhon was close to the dais and the princess noticed him, their eyes met, and she blushed. Typhon loved the white against that faint pink body.

Typhon reached the King's formidable throne. It was high up above him and he stared up at the King's knees.

"Yes, Son?" a deep voice echoed down.

"I'm here to ask for your daughter Hope's hand, my King of another land. I am Prince Typhon…"

"NO! Absolutely not! We will be finding her a suitor and it certainly will not be a Half-Elven scoundrel. Go back to your own country and dally with girls there. Now go!"

King Tobias quickly stood and put his fine riding boot to Typhon's chest and kicked him back down the dais stairs and Typhon landed on his arse and everyone around him backed away as he sprawled haphazardly on the marble floor. The partygoers made Typhon the laughingstock of the party. Donovan was especially pleased. The princess slipped away and went to the gardens to be alone. Both Typhon and Donovan noticed and followed.

Hope ran out into the gardens and cried. She couldn't believe her father embarrassed her like that. *What nerve! And Typhon is a Prince? He's perfect for me.* No doubts. She was muddled in her head and didn't hear the footsteps behind her.

"Hope?" whispered Typhon. He gently touched her shoulder.

She started. "Typhon!" she whispered back.

"Follow me," Typhon said. He took her deep into the garden where it was dark.

They sat on a bench together and immediately Hope reached out for him. She leaned into him. She smelled of roses. "I have urgent news," Typhon said as the glow erupted and outlined both of their bodies, "we're meant to be together. We're bonding through an ancient Elven magic. See the glow?" He held up his hand to show her. She pressed her lips to his and put her slender arms around his neck and pulled him to her. Their kiss lit a fire in her belly. He held her as she passionately explored his mouth with her little pink tongue. She slid onto his lap and straddled his hips. He groaned as her body rubbed against his. She leaned back and took note of his reaction. Hope watched his eyes carefully as she ground her bottom and hips across his lap. His eyes widened, darkened.

"Hope. I'm...I can't..." She cut him off and pushed even harder against him. His eyes widened then fluttered shut. Hope did it a third time and felt his hardness against her. Her mouth fell open, and she stopped moving. "Oh no you don't." Typhon whispered. He put his hands on her hips and pressed against her body.

She leaned into his mouth and their passion exploded. Her hands explored his chest, back, and shoulders. He secured his arm around her and trailed his other arm between them. He lifted the front of her skirts. He sought her out and realized her panties were open between her legs. His fingers danced and toyed with her and then he found his target. He gently stroked her. Hope panted in his mouth. She was ready for him. Typhon removed his hand and started untying his pants. When he was freed. He pulled away from Hope and looked her in the eyes.

"Are you sure?"

"Yes, Typhon. Only you."

He'd waited, longed to hear those words. Typhon helped her lift and then he laid her out, skirts hiked to her waist, on the bench. He took a second to admire her. Typhon positioned himself over her and then searing pain tore through his side as his blood went everywhere.

Typhon gasped then lost his breath and fell off the bench onto the concrete pathway. Hope sat up. She saw a figure with a bloody short sword pull back a blade and put it away.

She opened her mouth to scream, but a gloved hand quickly covered her mouth. "May I remind you, Highness, that you will be ruined if you are found out? Keep your mouth shut. He will live. Come with me, or I will kill him. Your choice." She could smell Typhon's lifeblood on her, and her body trembled. Tears hit her hair and fell like lonely raindrops on her now pink and red-stained bodice.

She got on the rider's horse that was hiding nearby. He put her in front so that he could hold her in his arms. He *finally* had her. Donovan was elated. They rode swiftly through the night, without stopping. Hope felt his tight embrace around her midsection and tried to calm her nerves. She dreamed he was Typhon holding her. Her eyes closed and after a few minutes, she found herself relaxed. Donovan almost jumped in the saddle when she leaned back against his chest. The smell of the ringlets of white roses in her hair overwhelmed him. He would never let that rakehell Typhon touch her again. After an hour or so he noticed that her body held a dim white glow. He dipped his head to her right ear.

"You're positively glowing, Milady."

Hope shivered at the influx of his warm breath over her sensitive pointed ear. The look that got from Donovan was a cute lopsided grin. Something rarely shown. "Seriously, Milady, why are you glowing?"

"Because I should be with my soulmate, but you stole me from him!"

That stung worse than any dagger's wound could. *Did she love Typhon? Was he just prolonging the inevitable? Did he just...no. She would come to see in time that the rescue was the best for her.*

"There are a group of female Elves on the road ahead. I don't get a good feeling from them. Please don't stop." Hope said.

Donovan sped his mare onward right past them. The females looked dour to see them pass without stopping. They were dressed like rangers and scouts. There were four in total. They had weapons but nothing out of the ordinary for their garb. Bows, short swords, daggers. Donovan kept it to memory in case he needed it for later and turned his attention back to Hope.

"I wasn't planning on stopping. How did you know that something was amiss?"

"I don't really know. I just felt it. Th-thank you for listening to me."

He hugged her tightly against him. "I will always listen to you, Hope."

"Really? Then, stop this instant and take me back!" She elbowed him in the stomach, hard, and he pulled back on the reins. The horse reared up and both fell, the dewy grass and stones caught them. Hope began to cry and rubbed her arm. Donovan, unhurt except for his pride, ran to her.

"Let me see," he inspected her arm and realized she'd broken it. He looked around for a good stick and then tore his own cloak and wrapped her arm and made a splint. "I'm going to get you to a healer. Let me help you back on the horse. Please don't fight me this time."

"I won't. I promise." Hope said sheepishly. She realized if he was going to hurt her, he could have by now, so she nestled deeply into his chest and tried to sleep.

Chapter Four

B ack in the gardens, Rose looked for Hope and knew Typhon was with her. She had a nose for these things after all. When she spied blood underneath some white roses, she undid the illusion and was dressed in all black and drew one dagger and one serrated short sword and silently slipped forward. She found the prince bleeding out but no princess. She kept the sword out and leaned down and placed her hand on Typhon and called to her god, the Faceless One, to heal him. Typhon's wounds slowly closed. Roselily touched her bracelet and informed Tobias of the scene she'd found. In no time flat, King Tobias came bounding out there, enraged. He picked up Typhon and held him up until he came to.

"Wha-what? King Tobias? Your Royal Highness. Oh gods, I'm naked and I'm bleeding on your boots."

"Boy, I told you to leave my daughter alone and look at you. I should have you strung and quartered for what you've done. Now, what have you done with Hope? Where is she?"

"I don't know."

A serrated blade went to his family jewels. His voice went up several octaves. "I swear I don't know! I got stabbed by someone and when I came to you were the first person I saw."

"He's not lying, your Majesty." Roselily said.

Tobias dropped the man on his arse and disdainfully looked away. "You owe me your life, boy. You have no idea how much trouble you're in. Get dressed."

"I swear on my mother, I'll get her back for you safely." Typhon stated.

"Oh really? Then I hold you to that. You'll go alone. Equip yourself in our armory and general store and be on your way post haste. She better be back completely unharmed, or I'll have your life in place of hers."

Typhon finished dressing. He looked at the King and knelt before him. "I give you my solemn vow that I will return your daughter unharmed."

"Rise, I accept your solemnity." King Tobias said.

Typhon headed towards the armory. He gathered chain mail, and leathers. Then, he stocked supplies for himself and a horse. He chose a fine Elven steed from the stables. He then bid farewell to the capital of Rosedale. Roselily met him at the gates.

"Typhon, take the south road out, that's where my senses tracked his horse. I hope that helps."

"Thanks. And thanks for healing me back there. I know it was you. The King would've let me die."

"I know," she winked, "now go, and bring her back alive." Typhon made a silent prayer to all the good gods that he could do just that. He took off on his horse at top speed and rode for hours throughout the night until he was so exhausted from the day's happenings that he had to camp for the night.

Hope jerked awake and didn't recognize her surroundings. She was in a soft, silky luxurious bed with a canopy. Her slippers were off. Her arm was healed. She felt no pain. She sat up and put her feet on the floor and looked around as she spied the door. Hope got up and walked around the room towards the door then Donovan stepped out of the shadows in her way, and they bumped bodies.

"Where are you going, Milady?" he asked.

"I...I was..."

His eyes were full of humor as he waited for an answer.

"Trying to escape?"

"Yes." She said and stomped her foot.

"That's not going to happen. You slept for eight hours of our journey. You would be completely lost out there. I won't let anything happen to you. I gave you my word."

She stared into his shadowy face with a disgruntled look. Their eyes locked. Her grimace slowly faded. They just stood there for a moment forgetting they were enemies. He leaned in slowly, carefully towards her lips. Taking his time, she was transfixed. Her gaze flicked to his mouth and back to his eyes. His lips gently met hers. Just one simple kiss.

Hope hauled back and slapped him on the cheek. She kicked him in the shin. Then she screamed. She'd hurt her foot. The girl Elf was bouncing around holding her foot. He stared at her and shook his head. She growled and came at him again; this time she raked her nails down his chest.

"Oh, my gods, Hope, stop, all I did was kiss you!" He caught her hands when she tried again. He put them behind her back and brought her directly to him and pressed her body up against the canopy post and pushed his half-naked body against hers. He was aggravated.

Her mouth dropped open. "Don't touch me, you scoundrel."

"I must keep myself safe from you somehow. Do I need to tie you up?"

She looked terrified. She gulped. "N...No."

"Then play nice."

"What are you going to do to me?" Hope said, her eyes wide.

"Nothing you don't ask for."

"I would never ask you for anything you...you..."

His eyebrow arched. "Ah, ah, ah. Play nice, Hope."

She struggled against him. Then, she kneed him in the crotch. He doubled over and went down. She flew to the door, but it was somehow locked against escape from the inside, and there were no windows. She felt trapped.

She stood and shook in a mix of fear and rage. "If you're going to ravish me, just get it over with."

Donovan's face was pained. He looked at her and laughed. "That's hardly my plans, Princess."

"Then, what *do* you want?"

"I want you to kiss me like you love me. Just once."

"What? No!"

"Yes. Anything more you will have to ask for."

"Well, that is not going to happen."

He walked over to her. She looked into his eyes again. She could see them clearly. A dark, almost black color. She admitted to herself that Donovan was quite handsome, but he was also insufferable, so that messed up the handsome. She wasn't quite sure what he meant by one kiss.

He slipped his arms around her back and pulled her close. His body heat mingled with hers. They were nose-to-nose, both breathing raggedly. She was nervous. He was turned on. He leaned down and touched her lips with his. She froze. Donovan could tell Hope was afraid. He pulled back and whispered, "Trust me," into her lips. He picked her lithe form up and strode to the bed. He laid her down.

Donovan crawled on top of her. He settled himself between her legs. He placed her hands around his neck. Hope's eyes widened.

Hope tried to lay still, but the increased pressure below from Donovan sent odd sensations through her. Her little pink tongue wet her lips subconsciously. That was Donovan's undoing. He dipped down and with a little effort he felt the tip of her tongue on his. Donovan pressed his hips into hers. Hope's mouth fell open. He deepened their kiss. He realized he was losing control. He quickly sat up and moved away from her. She stared at him, confused.

"Am I revolting to you?" she asked, curious.

He faced away from her, focused on his breathing. "No. I didn't want to do anything but kiss you, remember?" He felt her warm hand on his shoulder.

"Will you look at me then?"

"I think it's better if I leave right now." With that, he strode out of the room and locked it behind him.

Hope sat and stared at the door. She didn't like being treated this way.

Donovan went to his quarters and paced. *I was so close, too close. I'm not an infant. I should be more careful.* His breath would not slow. He was overly excited. He walked out of his rooms to head down the stairs to leave. He smelled it. Blood. *Her blood.* He took the stairs two at a time and made it to her door and unlocked it in no time.

"What's wrong, Hope?"

She looked at him with wide eyes. Hope stood by the bed and wiped her mouth. She had blood on her fingertips. "I bit my mouth open by accident. Wait, how did you..."

He was in front of her in a second, his mouth on hers. He slammed them both up against the wall in seconds and kissed her. He sucked her blood into his mouth and reveled in its taste. His need for her blood was nowhere near satisfied, so he sucked and pulled on her lip. Hope clung to his neck. She felt dizzy. He kissed down the side of her face and to her shoulder blade. He moaned loudly and his pants strained. At that same moment, he bit into her soft skin. She cried out in pain as his fangs grew inside of her flesh. He drank in her essence, long and deep. His body longed for release, for her, to make them one. She had tears streaming down her face. He lifted his fangs, sated, and licked her wound closed.

"Hope?"

She looked at him, her blood on his mouth, his eyes glowed ruby red. Her eyes ran him up and down and stopped on his large manhood. She tried to run past him and out the door, but he snatched her and tossed her on the bed. Her dress flew up to her waist and revealed her sexy underclothes. He saw them, and then she screamed as he ripped her dress off and tossed it aside.

"By the gods, why hide such beauty?" he begged. He discarded his pants. Her eyes widened. He crawled on the bed after her. She backpedaled. Her head hit the wall, and he crawled up her body. He took her into his arms and kissed her. The blood mingled between them. He gently peeled down her negligee. Tears streamed down her flushed cheeks. She was finally completely naked before him. He began deeply kissing her again. Hope was terrified not to comply. He pressed towards her several times. The last time he pressed he realized he could enter her. "I told you I wouldn't." he said over her lips. He flipped them over and sat her on top. He wanted to see what she would do. She stared at him, met his eyes, and glanced at how hard he was.

"No, please don't." she begged.

He loved that her hair had fallen out of the ringlets. It was pure cornsilk and past her waist. With the blood stains on her body and the look in her eyes, she no longer resembled a chaste princess. He wanted so much to turn her. Then she would only want him.

Hope crawled off him and put her face in her hands and hid her tears. Donovan felt horrible. He put on his tunic and looked at her.

"I'm sorry, Princess. I didn't mean to scare you. The last thing I want to do is hurt you." With that, he left the room, the lock clicked a second after the door shut.

She was starting to glow like before. She had mentioned something about bonding. That was an Elven love thing. Very ancient. Was it happening between them? Even between an Elf and an Elf turned Dread Vampire?

Chapter Five

♥

The next morning Hope woke up to roses all over the room in different colors. She found a breakfast tray that was so big and packed with food and drinks she couldn't decide what to try first. She was delighted. There was a window with curtains open. She marveled at that. It wasn't there last night.

She looked around for Donovan. He wasn't there. The door opened and remained open. Donovan came in.

"Good morning. How are you feeling this morning?"

"Do you have a library?"

"Yes. An extensive one, at your disposal."

"I'd like to see it. I need to research something."

"Of course. Let's eat and we'll head there straight away."

Hope had had a strange dream of being kidnapped several times over and brutally taken advantage of. She was unsettled by it. The word "Star Seed" echoed in her mind. She ate her breakfast. It was excellent. She pulled her negligee back on.

"Go open the closet, Hope. You are not going about in my castle dressed in that."

Hope found a closet full of beautiful silken gowns. She picked a sapphire blue to match her eyes. When she was dressed, she realized that except for the main body area, it was see-through, but she loved the luxurious feel of the silk, so she didn't mind.

She followed Donovan to his library. She stopped at the alphabetical letter of 'S' and began looking for ancient history books on Elves. She found several and gathered them to her bosom like newborn babies. Donovan stood behind her and kissed her on the neck while holding her close. He couldn't seem to take his hands off her for any length of time. She flipped through each page of each book until finally the last book had what she needed. She replaced the others on the shelf and said, "We can go now. I'll take this one with me for a while."

"I think I like it right here." He propped her up on the table and took her cheeks into his hands. He saw her bare neck. He licked his lips. He felt his fangs showing. He pulled her to him and held her close. She looked up at him.

"You need blood again." She said. Their eyes met. He silently nodded. She bared her neck and shoulder to him. "Go ahead."

"No, it hurts you. I know that it does."

She gently pulled his face to her neck. His lips were right over her pulse point. He smelled her virgin blood. Donovan kissed her neck, licked it, and as slowly as he could manage, pushed his fangs into her skin. She winced and squeezed her eyes shut. Donovan was instantly turned on and wanted her so badly. The curse of drinking virgin blood. He fed on her as his senses soared and he felt revitalized. He licked the wounds closed. Donovan was so grateful to Hope for this. He was about to say so when he saw something strange in her eyes. She looked pained.

"What is it?"

"I don't know. I...oooooh!" She wavered and he caught her before she fell. Her eyes squeezed shut. She shifted uncomfortably. Hope groaned aloud.

He watched her carefully. She panted softly.

"What do you need?"

"It...it's on fire!" she blushed crimson and touched her lower belly.

"Let me help. Trust me, ok?"

She nodded; eyes still shut.

He took a ragged breath knowing he had to maintain control. Donovan put two fingers between her womanly folds and teased her, rubbed her, felt her swell to his touch. As soon as he touched her, Hope's body arched, and she fell into his arms.

"Oh yes, Hope. Come for me. Relax and show me you love my touch."

He whispered to her in her ear. He coaxed her along until she squirmed and bucked beneath him.

Donovan's manhood was pulsing. He needed her. He spread her legs wide and bent down before her. Donovan then pressed his tongue to her. He traced circles and sucked on her until she came all over him. Hope was delirious. She mewled and screamed her pleasure. Donovan shook with need. He took his manhood in his hand and pleasured himself while he continued to pleasure her with his tongue. How badly he wanted to plant his seed in her! He knew all he had to do was thrust once and he would claim her. Fantasies danced in his head.

"I want you, Hope. I am in pain from need." He whispered.

She groaned his name and he stiffened more.

He stepped away and stood by the door. He pleased himself quickly. He wanted it over with. Hope sat up and watched. Their eyes locked and he let her watch him. When he came, he moaned so loud and looked into her eyes. Her body outlined in white glimmer. He smiled at her.

"Donovan? Are you all right?"

"Yes. I need rest. You should rest too."

Typhon had finally found the way to the Darkblades Castle. He snuck in through the side gardens expertly. He waited until the servants left the door open as they went to fetch water from the well. Then, he slipped in the side door and his senses were overwhelmed. He felt Hope's pleasure. He was confused. His stomach flipped and he became engorged with need for the princess, for his mate. It took ten seconds, and his arousal became rage. *Donovan!* Donovan was touching his mate! Typhon followed Hope's senses as they grew stronger, and he ran through the hallways until he came to a hallway where he had heard her cries of passion. He flew through the half-open doorway long sword drawn ready to kill Donovan. What he saw broke his heart. Hope flushed and disheveled. Donovan naked. The smell of sex in the air.

"DONOVAN!"

"C'mon you scoundrel. You came this far to die when I let you live once for the Lady's sake. I won't make that mistake again." Donovan's eyes narrowed to slits when he saw Typhon was glowing.

"You might have got to her first, but she still loves me. I know it. Don't you sweetling?"

Her two loves were about to kill each other, and she didn't know what to do.

Donovan looked at her. "Do you still have feelings for him?"

She didn't answer.

"Answer me!" he boomed.

"Don't yell at her!" Typhon advanced and struck Donovan hard with his longsword knocking him backward drawing blood in a clean slice across the forearm.

Hope winced in pain. A cut appeared in the same spot as Donovan's. She bled down her body. Donovan stabbed Typhon in the ribs. Typhon winced in great pain and staggered back. Hope coughed and doubled over as blood bubbled between her fingers. Both men looked at her at once. They forgot about the fight and ran over to her.

"Am I going to die? I can hardly breathe." Hope coughed again and blood ran out of her mouth. She passed out.

Chapter Six

♥

When Hope came to, she was lying in her bed, completely healed and both men were on either side of her by the bed. They both talked at the same time. Twice. Then both laughed nervously.

Typhon looked at her, "I'm so sorry, sweetling. I didn't know that we were connected in death as well as life. Donovan and I have worked through our problems, and we won't fight anymore. We promise."

"Really?" Her eyebrows went up. They both nodded. She hugged them both. "I love you both so much."

"Well, see, that's the problem. Hope, you need to choose." Donovan stated.

"No, I don't."

Donovan's voice went dark. "*Yes*, you do."

"I've bonded with both of you, at least almost. I refuse to choose. In Rosedale you can have up to three mates. I choose both of you, and I have that authority as a royal."

"I'm not arguing." Typhon said.

Hope turned to Donovan. "Please."

"I'll do it, but I don't like it."

That night after they all had a good time at supper. They laughed and joked together. All three slept in her big bed. The men shared her sweet lips. Neither pressed her for intimacy, nor did they approach the subject. It was a pleasant evening.

Hope had another frightening dream. She escaped to the library in the middle of the night to retrieve her book. She sat her candle down and found the place she had marked. She began to read. What she found out both amazed and scared her. The book fell from her hands. She trembled in fright. Strong arms encircled her from behind. She was startled. Hope turned around. Typhon smiled at her, then frowned.

"What is it? Talk to me."

"Don't ever let me go, Typhon." She clung to him.

"Never," He leaned down and kissed her forehead. He picked up her book. She snatched it away from his hands. "You okay?"

"Yes. Let's go back to bed."

The next morning Donovan woke up his new family.

"Let's eat." Donovan announced. He went to the door and brought in a set of trays full of eggs, bacon, sausages, breads, butters, jams, and juices, even coffee for Typhon.

"Was this just a guess, or did you know I liked coffee?" Typhon asked.

"Well, it's the number one export of your country. I figured you probably drank it. I know it's well-loved by your country."

Typhon nodded. "Good guess. I appreciate the gesture, Donovan. Now," Typhon said, drawing a deep breath, "there's something we all need to talk about. Hope is a Star Seed."

Hope's fork clattered to her plate, her hands shaking.

"My mother is an enchantress. She knows about these things. Star Seeds are only born once every few centuries. If anyone knew you could bear immortal children with inherent magical ability, they would...I don't want to think about it. Being able to bond with your soulmates is one of the signs. The second sign is you go through pregnancy very fast. The third sign is that you have intuition unlike any other, but that's where the ancient text stopped its description."

Chapter Seven

♥

Donovan listened carefully. He was right on all accounts, at least those he had seen so far.

"Then we will remain here, and I will hire more guards from the Temple of Asani. No one messes with them. And no one will mess with Hope as long as I live."

Typhon winked at Hope. "You have both of us protecting you, Princess. You're going to be just fine. We could take her to my country and stay at the castle where we'd have guards, magic, and priests protecting us. Not to mention the strongest Enchantress in the known world."

Donovan looked at Hope. "It's up to you."

Hope looked down. "I think I want to go to St. James. I'm sorry, Donovan."

Donovan said, "No apologies. It's wherever you want. I'll begin preparations now. I'll be back soon. Gather your things."

Typhon held his right hand up to look at it. A large golden ring with a sparkling ruby and the letters "SJ" in gold inlaid beneath the ruby. He talked into the ring. "Mother." He waited.

A soft feminine voice answered, "Yes, son? Is everything alright?"

"Yes, everything's perfect. Hope and Donovan and I are heading home."

"Who's Donovan?"

"My other spouse," he sighed.

Twinkling laughter and a snort as only his mom could produce made Typhon blush. Hope's eyebrows shot up. Hope giggled at him too.

"She couldn't choose, so she chose you both. I think I'm going to like this girl." Ilyanna said, an obvious grin in her voice.

"Now, we have two ways to travel. My mother can come and get us, and we can bypass all dangers, or we can travel in a carriage and hope for the best. We'll have to go through Rosedale though." Typhon grimaced.

Hope was quiet for a moment. Then said, "I'd like to go with your mother Typhon."

"What? What do you mean there's some kind of barrier? That's impossible. Yes, we'll be safe. We'll see you soon." Typhon nearly shouted into his ring.

Donovan stood. "What?"

Typhon looked at them both one at a time. "My mother said there's a magical or some sort of barrier blocking magic from here to St. James, perhaps further. She can't get her teleportation circle to work. It looks like we're going the old-fashioned way."

Donovan looked at Typhon, "Then guard her while I continue preparing. We'll set out tomorrow. At least magic creatures won't bother us."

Hope was nervous. She trembled from anxiety. One of her biggest skills was magic. If something or someone was blocking it off, then that meant she was useless in a fight and couldn't protect herself if both men went down. The thought made her shudder.

Chapter Eight

♥

L ater that same morning as they were preparing to leave and had
gotten horses and guards and a wagon, the trio heard a strange
audible pop.

"Mother? How did you get here, and in here?"

A beautiful sunbeam of an Elf turned around. She had the look
of Typhon, same hair, same eyes. Robes of red. *Interesting.* Hope
thought.

"Well, I've come to get you. I had a bad feeling. I did some research
and bypassed regular magic and surfed the wild magic that runs inherently on these parts and ours. First things first, I want to check on
Hope."

Typhon told his mother everything.

"Get your things and put a hand on my back." Illyanna stated.

They did as they were told. Hope realized she was finally leaving
her captivity room. Illyana cast the spell and time and space distorted
causing Hope to get nauseated. She let go covering her mouth, not
thinking, because her other hand was full. Typhon, Donovan and
Illyanna arrived without Hope.

Illyana turned around and panicked. "She let go, Typhon."

"What does that mean, Mother? Tell me."

"She's lost somewhere in the world by herself, and it is possible that she will be unable to use her magic to defend herself."

Chapter Nine

♥

Hope landed in a field. No houses nearby. Nothing. She walked off in a random direction. She realized her mistake in letting go and now she was lost somewhere and needed shelter. She spied a path through the woods and decided to follow. After about ten miles, she came across a large manor house. She decided to try her luck. She knocked on the door.

The front door opened. A very sensual-looking Elf stood in front of her, wearing only lace-up riding pants, with the laces part way undone, showing a bit too much. Long black hair, blue eyes, chiseled face and a very nice chest and arms.

"Hi there. How can I help you?"

"I-I need lodgings for the night if at all possible."

"Sure dear. Come on in. Let me get your bags."

She stood just inside the doorway. It was a marvelous place. Antique furnishings, plush carpets, no expense spared to make it...sensuous.

"Yoo-hoo. I'll show you to your room. It's up here."

"Oh sorry. I was admiring your home."

He took her to a room with a heart-shaped bed. She looked at it and then looked at him waiting for an explanation. He gave none.

"Do you need a bath? Follow me." He took her to a full-size spa and bath.

"Oh, I'd love one."

"Your soaps, bubbles, towels, everything are already in there. I'll have my cook make us supper and I'll see you in your room after, ok? You seem tired.

Gods, you're cute." He said as he walked off.

"Thank you for letting me stay the night. What is your name?"

"Uh...Chad in the common tongue. You can call me Chad."

Hope smiled back. His face morphed into Typhon's, then Donovan's. She heard Typhon's mother's voice.

"Hope, wake up. Wake up, Hope."

Hope's head swam. She couldn't see. Her hand went to her head quicker than a viper's strike. She heard herself moan. She blinked several times. Her head hurt. She slowly sat up. She was in soft grasses. *Where am I?* Hope surveyed the area and realized she was indeed in a field of high grass. She had just missed some rocks when she had fallen. She sat and pulled her feet in and began to weep softly thinking of Typhon and Donovan.

Typhon realized that Hope wasn't with them and immediately looked at his mother and said, "Please, Mother, find her."

"Already on it."

She sat in her divining chair next to a huge smokey quartz crystal ball and began to see shapes. "I've found her."

"Well, let's go!"

"No! I will go. You stay. I want to make sure she gets back this time."

Hope was curled up in the grass and then a shadow appeared over her. Hope started and almost screamed until she recognized Illyanna.

Hope got up quickly and swayed to and fro almost falling but Illyanna caught her.

"Be careful. Let's get home, dear. Now take your bag." Illyanna hoisted Hope into her arms leaving one arm free. Making several intricate hand gestures and saying unique magical words they faded from view. They showed up in Illyanna's library. Hope was let down gently on the couch and Typhon ran to her in giant leaps with Donovan behind him.

"My love! Are you ok?" He looked at her over and again.

"Yes, my head hurts and I feel like I might get sick from travel, but yes. Thank you, Illyanna, for finding me. I had given up."

"I will always find you. Never give up on me. We're bonded. I take that seriously. You are everything to me, Hope." Typhon placed kisses all over her face.

"Anyone who can capture my son's heart is priceless to me," Illyanna smiled.

"Thank you so much. I..." Hope fainted.

Illyanna checked her immediately. She began casting spell after spell. Typhon knew to be quiet and let her concentrate. Donovan cursed.

"Get a Priest, now." Illyanna seemed grim.

A Priest came in and checked on Hope. He turned to the trio and with sad eyes stated, "Princess Hope is in a magical sleep of some sort, but it's no magic that I've ever seen."

"Nor I" agreed Illyanna.

"I will be in here every hour to check on her. I suggest you make her as comfortable as possible then get some sleep. She's perfectly healthy, just in some sort of induced state of deep slumber." The Priest explained.

Chapter Ten

♥

"Great job, Alistar. We now have the location of my daughter, and you are psi-linked with her. Keep her asleep." Tobias Rosedale said.

"As long as His Royal Majesty gives me what I promised in the end." Alistar replied.

"Of course, Son. You will be a Rosedale, and you will have my daughter as your wife."

Tobias looked at his men. "Prepare the teleportation pad, and the Royal carriage, the large one." The men took off running.

Rosedale laughed until he cackled. It was all going according to plan.

They assembled the carriage, soldiers, wizards, and priests to take in an entourage.

Alistar was alone and began fantasizing about Hope. He had loved her since they were kids making mud pies together. His pants grew tight, and he gently rubbed himself trying to stop it. It just made it worse. Luckily, he was in the bathroom, and he saw the entrance to the girl's spa, and he walked in. He saw a fine, young Elf bathing. His lips twitched.

"Girl, come bathe me."

"My Lord Alistar?"

He lifted her naked body out of the water, pulled his pants down and pushed her against the wall. He entered her and began to steady his rhythm although it was difficult. Her lips curled upward in acceptance. They kissed for a long time. He could feel her contracting, coming for him. Her wetness was audible. He began kissing her neck and then bit her. Her body stiffened, relaxed, stiffened, relaxed. It was so hot. Alistar was careful not to take too much blood. He pressed in again and then abruptly stopped. He only wanted a baby with Hope, not some random girl. He carried her back to the pool.

"There. Wash yourself clean. Thank you."

She trembled. "Thank you."

He contacted the girl's mind and erased her memory of the event. She was left to wash up with no idea why she was trembling. Alistar did not care. She'd served a purpose. He was tired of using substitutes for Hope. His day was near. Alistar, triumphant, washed up and walked out and got into the carriage and waited for His King.

Tobias joined him several minutes later. He arched his brow and quipped, "You look smug."

Alistar chuckled. "Yes, well I availed myself of one of your servants."

Tobias' brow furrowed. "They're not all for your pleasure, you know."

"I erased her memory of it. Besides, I was thirsty."

"Speaking of thirsty," Tobias pulled out a bottle, and two glasses, "To victory, fresh virgin."

They clinked glasses and drank deep of the innocent blood within.

It didn't take long for the carriage to arrive at the warp area.

"When you get what you want, use this to signal me, Son-in-law." Tobias said and handed him a royal family signet ring.

Alistar's bright red-brown eyes widened. "Thank you, your Royal
–"

Tobias waved off the formalities. "Just do your part and you will
have my favor and my daughter."

The carriage zipped and wavered out of existence. When it came
back into the material plane it was a mile away from Castle St. James.
A surprise visit for sure.

Alistar scried inside the castle. Looking with his mind, not with
magic, and found exactly where Hope lay in complete peace. He licked
his lips and felt his top fangs growing, ready to feed. That wasn't all
that was ready on his body. The mere sight of her excited him. He quietly popped into the room. He restrained his unbridled passion, and
gently touched her forehead. The power transferred. He connected
to her mind. He erased all her memories and replaced them with new
ones. He gently lifted her up and envisioned the carriage again. He
shut his eyes and concentrated hard. They ended up in the carriage.
Alistar signaled to Tobias. Tobias looked at his ring. He sent a message
back.

"Make it quick. I'll be right back."

Alistar slid a wedding ring on her finger. He couldn't help himself.
He gently placed a kiss on her lips. He was in love instantly. His original
plan was to turn her into his spawn, and bed her, but for some reason
he couldn't and chose to wait until she asked.

Tobias walked right up to the palace invisibly. With Illyanna being
distracted the protection wards were weak. He mist-formed through
the door and found her and Typhon together. He waited for the
opportune moment. Typhon left. Tobias sneered. He was silent as
he approached her. He admired her beauty. He had never tasted a
sun-loving Elf before. He bore his fangs and captured her neck in a
bite and snaked his right arm around her arms and left hand over her

mouth. He felt her tension. She struggled but he overpowered her. He drank in a large swallow of her blood. He smiled as he drank another swallow. Tobias bit his wrist and forced it into her mouth. Illyanna tasted his blood. It was like fine Elven wine. She shook violently. Her mind swam. She felt his body pressed into hers from behind. Her eyes squeezed shut. She felt free, high, turned on, alive. Her skin tingled. Tobias knew she was his. He gently turned her around. He lifted her chin to look at him. Her eyes, now turning a beautiful ruby red, met his. He saw her tiny fangs. He held out his hand. She took it. They went back to the carriage.

Alistar stared in amazement at Illyanna who seemed to be under a spell. She was bloody and it made Alistar lick his lips. "Another ally against the St. James family and a new member of my own." Tobias stated happily as he motioned to Illyanna.

"Damn. You're unbelievably skilled. I'm highly impressed." Alistar said.

"Our family will rule everything one day soon. I'm building an empire." Tobias stated.

The carriage hurried along the path to the warp area to return to the Rosedale palace. They disappeared just as they had arrived. When time shifted and they were entering nil space Alistar happened to glance at Hope. She was glowing with bright white light. When they re-entered the material plane, the light ceased. He held her close to his body and wished she responded to him in kind.

The party of four arrived at the palace. Tobias left with Illyanna and told Alistar to be especially gentle with his daughter and that he expected them both at breakfast. Alistar gently lifted Hope into his arms. He carried her to his chambers. He laid her in his bed. Then, he slowly took the psionic induced sleep away until she started to stir.

He waited. Her eyes opened slightly, and she looked around and saw
Alistar. She smiled.

"Alistar, where am I? I feel so out of sorts."

"You took a fall, Princess. Just rest." He was hoping she wouldn't
notice his growing erection.

"Will you lay by me? I'm scared for some reason."

"Of course. Anything you want." He smiled at her. She scooted
over and he took his boots off and got into bed with her and then
started fumbling with his coat and shirt.

"Here, let me." She reached for his coat and helped him take it off,
then made quick work of the buttons on his shirt. When his upper
body was bare before her, she sucked in a breath. Then, she turned
away. Hope thought about how much he'd changed. He was built,
grown. Not the teenager she remembered. They had come close to
making love once as young ones, but Alistar had honor and stopped.
Now, Hope was wishing to touch his chest and see if he was real. She
turned over and let him snuggle her from behind. She noticed her
human wedding band. Alistar was human. She froze.

"Alistar?"

"Hmm?"

"Are you my husband?"

"Yes, love."

She turned around to face him. Their eyes met. "Why don't I
remember?"

"You fell off our horse coming from the outdoor wedding. You hit
your head hard. You've been out for almost two days."

"Oh. Sounds like me."

"It's not like you meant to. I was worried."

"Can...I touch you?" she asked, as she stumbled over her words.

He chuckled. "Of course. I'm all yours."

She splayed her hands and fingers on his chest and wound them in the hair. "You've grown up."

"So have you, my little Belle."

Her eyes widened. The last time he called her that was the night they almost made love. Their eyes met. Her hands stopped moving. He leaned down towards her. She tipped her chin up to meet him. Their lips touched and something sparked. They were frantically pulling and grabbing at each other. Their tongues delved deeply. He ripped her gown open. She gasped in his mouth but let it happen. He made quick work of his pants. Naked and touching each other desperately, Alistar knew he had to feed on her before she found out he was a vampire. His need was beyond anything he'd ever felt. Hope trembled in his arms, and he hadn't even touched her sensitive areas yet. He trailed a warm path of kisses down her neck to the crux of her shoulder. He licked, sucked, and then pulled her tightly to him and bit down. She tried to pull away. He drew in a long draught of her blood. It felt like liquid lightning. She was pure. His senses were heightened. Alastair's one fault was his inability to control his bloodlust. Hope's body went limp against his. Every impulse screamed to drain her, kill her. He released her, and she fell against the bed out cold.

Chapter Eleven

♥

Typhon alerted his father to everything that happened, and the King looked empathetic. He hugged his son. "It is going to be alright somehow. We will not stop until we have the answers we seek, and your wife is restored to health."

Typhon nodded. That was all he needed to hear. He trusted his father. He went back up to tell his mother and when he entered the room, shock and anger sent his senses reeling.

"Where's the Princess?!" He shouted.

The servants looked perplexed. "I thought she was moved?" one said.

Typhon roared in anger. He ran back to his rooms and everywhere else checking for his mother and mate. He alerted the guards. Typhon was beside himself. He found his father and through gasps of air told him. The guards were filling the room in twos.

"Your Highness we must put you under lockdown so that your safety is assured. This is obviously an attack."

"Oh, bloody hells! Nothing like this has ever occurred here before. What happened to your mother's wards?"

Typhon looked grim. "Father, she's gone. She was either kidnapped against her will or killed. There was blood all over the floor."

Typhon left the room headed for his mother's scrying ball. He knew how to use it but didn't like to. He put his hand on it. "Show me Illyanna St. James." Nothing. "Show me Hope St. James" Still nothing.

Suddenly, from behind him he heard "I told you I didn't trust you from the start. Let's go after Hope."

Typhon stood, turned around, and punched Donovan across the room into a bookcase. "Right now, I hate you!"

Donovan twisted and rubbed his jaw. He climbed out of the dusty books. "You're just mad. You will get over it. I'm here to help."

"How the nine hells do you know what is going on?"

"I am not sure," he looked into Typhon's eyes, "But I think it has something to do with that Elvish bond."

"Us...fucking weird. Whatever. Let's get our Princess back."

"Yeah. Her father was responsible for both kidnappings. Whether your mother is alive, I do not know, but the last time I felt the connection to Hope was a day ago." Donovan said.

"You mean, we got to fight Rosedale to get them back? That's insanity. We are no match for the military strength of Rosedale."

"Both of our countries together would pose a credible threat. You and I could sneak into the palace while the attack on the capital took place. That's the one weak point in their defenses, Rosedale Harbor is open on three sides." Donovan said.

"All right. I'm in. Let's plan." Typhon said.

That night Typhon slept in an unfamiliar bed, and it made him have nightmares and toss and turn. Halfway through the night, Typhon awoke to Donovan standing over him with a lantern.

"You okay, man?" Donovan asked.

"No, I can't get comfortable."

"It's more than that. I shared your nightmares."

Donovan sat on the side of the bed.

Typhon looked down, "I feel pretty stupid, but I need her all the time."

"Me too."

Donovan's eyes met his. "You're my bonded mate too."

Donovan put the lantern on the floor. When he turned back, Typhon had moved closer. He held his breath. Typhon leaned in and gently, as if scared, tried to kiss Donovan. Donovan moaned softly. It felt familiar and good. Typhon laid Donovan underneath him and undid his pants and tossed them aside. He was gentle as he pressed inside of him. Donovan's head fell back, and his mouth opened in delight. Typhon caught his mouth in a tongue-filled kiss. Typhon showed Donovan his loving side, kissing up and down his neck, his ears, filling Donovan with shivers. They made love for hours. They felt the familiar and safe bonding energy envelope them. Typhon showed Donovan the meaning of lovemaking when after finishing deep inside him he took Donovan into his mouth allowing him to finish. Afterward, they slept in each other's arms contented.

The next morning, they kissed hello and bathed together and had breakfast. They went to the war room to hash out a plan to get Hope out and Typhon's mother back. Over a map of the Darkblades and Rosedale areas they plotted their troop locations. They both decided to storm the Castle Rosedale with a Priest, a Sorcerer, and twenty of the elite guards. They would take the little-known back exit and storm the castle looking for both Elven women.

"Do you think he has them in the dungeons?" Donovan asked.

"No. my mother once told me that key prisoners are treated like royalty in the Rosedale Kingdom. It's part of the King's twisted game to make them like him."

"That's sadistic." Donovan made a face.

"He's sadistic from what I've heard."

"We need to get moving. I don't want her there any longer." Donovan seemed nervous.

Typhon put a hand on his shoulder. "I know, I feel it too. An anxiety that we can't feel our bond with her. At least it was nice last night feeling the bond with you. I needed it."

Donovan reached for him and kissed him. His kiss was desperate.

Typhon held him close to his body. Donovan was truly suffering, and he felt it. It matched his own feelings. The familiar glow burst around them.

Typhon groaned but pulled back from the kiss. "Later tonight then? First, we must get everything in order. I want to leave tomorrow."

"Yes. Yes. Exactly. I'll take you up on your offer for later. I cannot resist you."

Typhon smiled. "I know the feeling."

"I know you do." Donovan grinned.

Chapter Twelve

♥

They secured their personal entourage and shared plans with them. Then, the Darkblades army was put on high alert and told they would be moving into attack phase tomorrow morning for a surprise attack on the Rosedale Capital.

"You will not kill women and children. However, put to death any able-bodied man you come across that draws a weapon on you or poses a threat. The goal is to fight your way to the palace and surround it and fight the guards until they surrender. If anyone surrenders take them as prisoners. Now, be ready. Rosedale is a sadistic piece of horse shit. Don't doubt he will play dirty and there will be no rules on his end. If you follow what I've said here, I give you leave to decide what methods of killing and violence you will use to survive. I suggest taking all and any magical weapons and armor, for you will be fighting against them. It is no secret Rosedale is wealthy. If you capture a member of the royal family do not kill him or her. We will use them for our own bargaining. Good luck and there will be a special military blessing for you tonight at seven. May the Gods bless us and keep us safe."

The men and women of Donovan's army roared in approval. Weapons clanked together. The sound was deafening.

Donovan nodded once and walked off with Typhon. "What do you want to do now?" Donovan asked Typhon. Typhon grinned at him. Donovan felt his pants tighten hearing Typhon's thoughts.

It was King Tobias' idea to make a superior form of each race using his daughter's powers. The Elves would be the most lithe, powerful in bow and sword. The Half-Elven would produce the best of both races. Once this was accomplished, he would produce an army that couldn't be beaten. His plan was perfect. The only problem that both he and Alistar could foresee is Hope might not remain under their sway long enough to create this army. Alistar would proudly father all the Half-Elven soldiers. Tobias hadn't picked the Elven lover for her yet, but Alistar was already dreading it. He wallowed in his misery, and there was a knock at their door. Alistair cracked the door open. A younger, attractive male Elf stood there.

"I'm here to take the princess to start the Royal plan. I go first according to this decree." He handed it to Alistar. Alistar looked the document over and in sorrow woke up his wife.

"Please go with this Elf. He needs your assistance in Royal duties."

"Um, okay." She seemed confused. She pulled on an elegant shift dress and shoes. When she saw him, she realized they were probably about the same age. She followed him. They came to a door, and he opened it for her. She walked in. Then turned to him. "What is going on?" she asked.

"Would you like some Elven wine?"

"Yes, please."

They sat at a table drinking together. "You are to be the ambassador of a special plan."

"What does it involve?" She rubbed her forehead. Elven wine normally didn't affect her this bad.

He just smiled at her. "Some fun things. Not a lot of difficult tasks."

She giggled uncontrollably and covered her mouth. He smiled at her again. He was so sexy. She was impressed by his black hair and blue eyes. He stood. She watched him carefully. He held out his hand. She took it and stood. In a sudden motion, his lips were on hers. She didn't protest. A sword blade came out through his chest in front of her. Her mouth fell open to scream, but nothing came out. She couldn't think, couldn't see very well. She heard Alistar's voice.

"Don't trust your father. Don't trust me. I would do anything to have you. He would do anything for more power, even sacrifice his own daughter in the mix. Take this," He handed her his personal signet ring, "and use it find Typhon."

They heard stomping and saw the King and his elite guard coming for them.

"Alastair what will happen to you?"

"I'm a traitor by letting you go."

She reached up and kissed him and turned the ring on her finger. Time melded into space. They came to in Typhon's bedroom. Before she could run off, Alastair finished their kiss. It was breathless, a prolonged goodbye, a love lost before it started. It surprised him to find he was tearing up and in need at the same time. Alastair ran beside her calling for Typhon. A guard regiment stopped.

"Princess? We've been scouring the castle. Their Lordships went to find you and the Queen. You were taken prisoner. Are you all right and who is this?" The guards all turned halberds out toward Alastair. Alastair froze.

"This is my best friend, Alastair. He rescued me. Lower your weapons."

"Your Highness it's best if we stay outside your room and balcony."

"Absolutely."

She took Alastair's hand and led him to her room. She sat on her favorite cushy chair. He sat across from her. She didn't feel well, but she didn't say anything. They sat there in awkward silence. This was the first time that Hope had ever felt odd around Alistar before.

She got up and paced the floor. Hope's cheeks flushed. She stopped, pointed at him, then closed her mouth and began pacing again. "I can't. I just can't. This is too much. You were my best friend." She stared at him, broken heart in her eyes.

He immediately went to her, "I was out of my mind wanting you." Alistair touched her cheek. She winced and pulled away.

"You've done enough. Do not touch me again. Go lick the bootstraps of my father. See where it gets you. You could have had me had you approached me even one time before I left the castle."

"I'm so sorry. Tell me how to make it right."

"You brought me home. I will spare your life."

Chapter Thirteen

♥

D onovan and Typhon set the troops into place about three
miles away from Rosedale Harbor. The two lords made their
way around the back of the palace and up through the tunnels that
Donovan knew about. The two men waited in the tunnels for all hell
to break loose. When they heard tell-tale signs of a large battle they
hurried along until they came to the servants' entryway. The servants
were shocked by the intrusion and went to ring the emergency bell.
Donovan expertly cut it down and sent it careening across the room
until it made a loud clang off the soup pot and into the soup it went.

"No one's going to get hurt. We're here to take back the Princess."

"And my mother," Typhon added. Donovan looked at the smallest
girl. She flushed pink to her ears. He gently lifted her chin to look him
in the eyes. "Sweety, which way are the bedrooms from here."

She pointed. He laid a quick kiss on her hand. The two men took
off running. They raced up the many circular flights of stairs.

"How many floors again?" Typhon asked, irritated.

They rounded the next set of stairs to find Illyanna in one of the
open bedrooms with three men surrounding her in various states of
dress.

"Mother, what the hell?!"

She turned to face them and then in an instant stood in front of them naked and unashamed, blood stains on her mouth and chin.

"Mother, did you just float over here?"

A stream of Elvish incantations spewed from Illyanna's mouth. Then, she screamed "DIE!" and pointed at Donovan. A white streak of magic struck him in the chest. His face contorted, and he looked at Typhon and grabbed his chest. He choked one last breath and fell into a slump. Typhon caught him and lowered him to the floor.

Typhon felt like a part of him was ripped away. "No, no, no, no." Donovan, his comrade, his love. "No, please, look at me. Donovan." He felt for breath and felt nothing. Typhon saw his mother draw power that signified another spell. He sprung back up and brought the hilt of his sword to Illyanna's temple and knocked her out cold. "She's a vampire now, so *that* was this family's secret of longevity." Typhon meticulously went through and broke all his mother's fingers in one ugly bend backward. He carried both out the way he came. Then he heard Hope's voice in his mind.

"Darling, tell me you're okay? I'm in your castle. Come home. I'm just fine."

"I'm on my way." He gently sat Donovan on his horse. He tied up his mother and put a gag in her mouth. He put her over the horse naked as she was. He didn't care. The fact that his mother was even capable of such an atrocity messed with his head and his heart. He rode off for the nearest area of wild magic to use Donovan's ring. Typhon lost all care for the battle. He wanted Hope back in his arms, his mother returned to normal, and Donovan alive.

He reached the wild magic area and turned Donovan's ring. He came back into the present in Hope's bedroom, still on horseback. A strange man was in the room. Typhon got off the horse and Hope grabbed his face and they kissed so hard that they were panting in seconds. He pulled back. Tears ran down his cheeks.

"Typhon?" she asked.

"Donovan's gone, honey. My mother killed him because she's been turned into a vampire."

"Oh, my GODS!" She fell back into the chair unable to stand. She wept bitter tears. Typhon lowered Donovan off the horse. Memories of his piercing eyes, his soft hair in her fingers, the morning her room was filled with flowers flooded her mind like torrents of rain. She forced herself to look at his lifeless body. His lids were shut. She would do anything to have him look at her one more time. She flung herself at Donovan. Holding his face, his skin felt cooler than normal, she placed kisses all over his cheeks, forehead and finally lips.

At that very moment, Typhon noticed his mother stirred. "The fuck you are..." He raised his sword hilt to knock her out and Alistair held him off and put a hand towards his mother. She fell to the floor with a thud.

"I'll hold her off, no problem. See to your woman." Alistair said.

Typhon nodded. He ran to Hope. "Beautiful, tell me you're all right. He held back her long hair. He wanted to shield her from this tragedy and whisk her away from here. Somewhere safe that they could say, "fuck everyone else." But where would that be? Alistair rushed into the room. He startled both. He pressed a ring into Typhon's hand.

"Run!" was all he could get out. He shut the door and Hope and Typhon heard the door to the bedroom burst open.

King Tobias yelled, "Traitor!" They heard Alistair scream. Hope looked at the ring and put her fingers on it. They faded from the location and showed up in Hope's secure bedroom at the Darkblades

Castle. She picked up the ring and cast a spell over it and it turned into ashes.

"Now he can't track us with that ring," She explained, "Your mother is a vampire; and my father is after me for some unknown reason other than he disapproves of our marriage."

"I still love you, Hope. Our bond is still strong. You feel it right?"

"Yes, I do. Even Alistair said he couldn't break it though he tried."

He covered her up and turned to leave to arrange their lodgings and guards, when she gently tugged his fingers. He went back to her.

"Yes, love?"

He wanted her so badly. Right when he was ready to turn her over and take her, he noticed she was sleeping. His face twisted in confusion. He began to miss his sarcastic Donovan. He imagined what he would say at a time like this, and his eyes welled up. He swore he'd kill Tobias. He deserved a cruel end. No mercy. He took Donovan and his mother away. Typhon sat in the bathroom and cried all alone.

Chapter Fourteen

♥

Back at the St. James palace things were coming undone at the seams. Tobias unleashed his entire family of wives, children and stepchildren, all Dread Vampires and the meanest and most tough, upon the palace guard. The guards' meager weapons did nothing to them, like toothpicks on steel. Claws rendered flesh, blood splattered across bodies and insane cries of pleasure and horrendous curdling screams of death mixed in the cacophony of the turning of the tides of war. The King St. James at the end of the fray came face to face with King Tobias. Tobias slashed him across the face with one clawed hand and the other came up to cut right through the royal seal hung about his neck. The seal clattered to the ground and Tobias stomped it into dust.

"Your Kingdom is at a ruin. Give in old man."

"I will go down fighting!" he huffed. The King St. James pulled his longsword high overhead. Just as he was about to bring it down upon Tobias' head, he faltered. In his sight, there was his wife, snapping the neck of one of his own guards, her body covered in blood, a wicked smile across her face. He lost every ounce of control he had left. He slashed his sword down on Tobias with all he had. Tobias caught it in mid-air and cackled. "You are my next meal. Your wife tasted particularly good."

"You bastard!"

St. James slid his blade down and cut Tobias in the hands and arms. Tobias' blood ran down his arms and seeped crimson into his riding shirt. Tobias reached forward in a flash and ripped the King's throat out. As the King of St. James gurgled and fell to the floor, two of King Tobias' sons brought forth the only daughter of the St. James family. Tobias, covered in the King's blood, realized he was not prepared for such a meeting.

"Take her to the palace. Prepare her room. Put guards at every exit. No windows. Give her whatever she needs to feel at ease. I will see to her personally later."

The young teen looked at the bloody carnage, bodies strewn everywhere, her father bloodied at her feet. She fainted into the arms of Lance, Tobias' eldest. His fangs dripped with the scent of her virgin blood.

"You are not to touch her until I allow it." The King demanded.

"Yes, Father." He picked Phaedra up in his arms and left the room.

"Now. My beautiful family feast upon the rest of the loyal guards. Turn those who offer fealty. Illyanna come to me, my sweet."

Typhon's mother came to Tobias. They kissed and shared blood. Tobias made a face.

"What is it my love?" Illyanna inquired.

Tobias gently placed his hand on her lower belly. He looked into her eyes. "You didn't tell me. Why? I would not have let you anywhere near the battle."

"I wanted to fight by your side."

"You're carrying my child."

"Yes."

"We will celebrate when we return home. For now, I want you out of the battle. Return home at once and look after Phaedra."

"If you insist."

"I insist."

"I love you, Illyanna."

"I am forever yours, Tobias."

The Rosedale family turned their attention to the floor littered with bodies. Tobias sneered. He picked up Donovan's lifeless body and bit into his neck, drinking deep. He put his hand over his heart to channel the dark life force back into Donovan. Donovan sputtered, choked, and wheezed. Donovan clung to Tobias. He couldn't stand.

"Bite me and live, Son." Donovan tried to bite Tobias in the same way but was so weak he couldn't break skin.

"Let it come. You're almost there, Donovan." Donovan felt a passion for life, a pleasure rush, he wanted more. He bit down hard on Tobias. The copper lifeforce filled his mouth. His body came alive. He felt like he could dance. Donovan lifted his head away and groaned.

"Oh gods, what is this?"

"Welcome back, Son." Tobias said and licked the wound closed on Donovan's neck. Tobias' daughter Marhi stood nearby and then hugged Donovan.

"Welcome to the family, Donovan."

"What do you need me to do, my King?"

"Help us take care of the rest of the guards. If they surrender, bite them, give them your blood. More allies." Tobias explained.

"Absolutely, my King."

Tobias smiled brightly at Donovan.

After the room's bodies were drained and turned the new army was sent off to finish the business ahead of them. Tobias stayed after they left. He turned to the limp, barely alive Alistair.

"Now, for you. You are a traitor. You deserve the worst of deaths, and so you shall have it." Tobias bit him and took in huge gulps of his blood until he was so weak, he collapsed against him.

"Mercy. Please."

Tobias cackled and looked deeply into his eyes. "You are getting mercy." Tobias drank from him until there was nothing left. Tobias watched as Alistair turned into a spawn. The transformation was painful. He lost his strength, vitality and any bodily functions he had left and became a lifeless corpse to forever wander the halls of St. James.

Tobias left him there to figure out his new fate, as he was no longer a threat to anyone. Tobias was ready to join the fray with his family. He was excited to fully join his daughter Hope to Donovan and build his vampire army now that he had them both under sway. He stopped for a minute. He thought of his daughter, Hope. Then, he sent a telepathic message to her.

"Daughter, come home. Donovan is safe and alive. Come to me. Come home." Hope heard her father's voice in her dreams. She stirred. Typhon watched her sleep from a chair across the room. Hope sat up and stretched. She crossed the space between them in seconds. She was on his lap. She took his face in her hands and kissed his lips.

Tobias instructed Donovan to retrieve his daughter from Castle Darkblades.

Donovan looked upon Tobias as a father-figure. Something Donovan never had.

Hope sat up on her elbows and looked at Typhon. "I feel Donovan nearby."

Typhon stopped. "That's impossible."

"No, love, he's alive."

They got up and went to find the head of the guards. Donovan stepped out in front of them. His eyes were glowing deep ruby.

"Hope, come home with me. You belong to me."

"Donovan, I don't want to live with my family."

"I'm your family."

Typhon moved Hope behind him. He stood, towering over Donovan.

"You are not taking her anywhere. You'll have to kill me first."

"Don't make me."

Hope was poisoned by the tiniest of darts. She started to fall backwards as hands slid around her midsection and moved her off into the shadows. They teleported to Hope's bed chamber at Rosedale Harbor palace. Typhon punched out at Donovan and hit nothing but air. Donovan sneered at him. The illusion faded.

After making a quick run of the St. James palace, the Rosedale family and the newly turned guards and townsfolk that didn't resist all went back to Rosedale Harbor to Tobias' castle. Once inside Tobias barked orders as to where the new troops should go and made concessions for the Elves to be given or built new homes in the city proper or the forest just outside the walls.

Chapter Fifteen

♥

Phaedra, Typhon's only sister, paced the floor in her room. Her nervousness was clear. She didn't know what to expect in this den of vampires, but it couldn't be good. Finally, after she had paced for several hours, the door opened. King Tobias and his son Lance walked in. They shut the door. Phaedra with her long cornsilk hair, slightly pointed ears and cerulean blue eyes, lithe body of a dancer, stood before them. She tried to be brave.

"I am the King. You are welcome here my dear. You will now be my ward since your parents have no kingdom. I am going to leave you in the capable hands of my son, Lance, and if you need anything he will get it for you."

Tobias left the room. Lance tried to keep it reigned in. His mouth watered from her scent; she was nervous, so it made it stronger. He wanted to rip her clothes off and ravage her. He was always the overbearing one. He had to be patient. She was only sixteen from what his father said.

"Well, nice to meet you." He started off.

She just stared at him. Their eyes met briefly, and she looked away quickly.

"Phaedra, look at me. I'm not going to hurt you."

"Yes, yes you are. You're going to kill me like my father."

"No, that was war between nations. You are a ward of Rosedale, like family."

"Then let me go."

"You'd be kidnapped or worse. No way."

"Better than staying here with you vampires."

Lance made a face. Her blood boiled from anger. His fangs began to grow and gods he couldn't help it. He tried to keep his mouth closed.

"Why are your eyes glowing?" she asked a simple innocent question. It set off the beast in him. He crossed the space between them in two large steps and scooped her up, even as she beat on him with fists, and he threw her on the bed. She bounced. He was on her in an instant. He pinned her arms down with his and his body, full clothed, covered the rest of her body. She couldn't move.

"No, please, don't..."

His lips covered hers. She gasped. His tongue delved into her mouth, touching hers. Phaedra felt his fangs. One wrong move and she could get cut. She'd never been kissed. He was pressing so hard against her she could barely breathe. She gasped for air. He slanted his lips a new way and touched her tongue again. Lance wanted her bad. He was fully hard. Her little pink lacey day dress was so thin he could claw it right off if he wanted to.

He leaned up a little, "Phaedra..." Her eyes widened. He just moaned her name. He pressed his hips into hers. Her mouth opened into an O as she felt his manhood pressing into her. She was nowhere near ready for this. "I want you Phaedra."

"Lance please, no."

"If I don't take you, I'm going to bite you. I can barely control myself right now."

"No! I want you to die, you vulgar beast."

Lance started to shake. His eyes shone a brilliant blue. Their eyes met. She was mesmerized. His fangs grew anew when he thought about sharing blood with her. He looked at her. "Do you want to be mine, Phaedra?"

Then, she saw his fangs. Fully out. His eyes were ruby red. She realized he was dangerous.

He yanked away from her in one fell swoop. He leaned against the wall and looked away. "Oh gods, girl. I need you. I'll lose control."

Phaedra held deathly still. "Please let's just be friends. I can't be anything to you. I don't want to be a vampire."

"You'll change your mind. Then, you will see what you're missing." He walked out the door and locked it outside. Phaedra let out a relieved sigh.

The next day the city of Rosedale counted its losses in the surprise attack from the Darkblades army. Donovan called an end to the attack and sent the army home. Some of the more impressive soldiers were captured and turned and then put into the ranks of Rosedale's guard.

Chapter Sixteen

Typhon received a magical letter in the form of Tobias' voice, and it stated: "I've got your mother, your Kingdom, and Donovan living here in the palace. I propose a truce. Come home to your family and Hope."

Typhon realized his fate was sealed. He would probably be killed.

He travelled to Rosedale by carriage. He went right to the throne room; the guards welcomed him in. The entire Rosedale family was gathered in the throne room. Hope felt uncomfortable. Her eyes flicked to Donovan. Then, back to her father. Tobias stepped up to Typhon. He held out his hand. Typhon shook it.

"I'll have the footmen bring your things around. Typhon your bedroom adjoins Hope's."

Hope showed Typhon the teleportation pad. They made it to her luxurious room and the footmen showed her in and showed Typhon his rooms. One footman locked the door quietly to keep Typhon out. Typhon tossed his fencing shirt in the corner, along with boots and stockings. He undid his riding pants loose and laid down and smelled something like lavender and fell asleep. Many hours passed. Typhon woke up sweating profusely in the pitch dark.

Hope had bad dreams. She tossed and turned. Hope padded across the lush, carpeted floor and tried to open Typhon's door. She gently pulled on the door and pouted like a child. *I just wanted to see him. This isn't fair.*

Chapter Seventeen

Typhon rose from the bed and tried to open the door between his and Hope's room. When it wouldn't budge, he dressed and then put a boot to the door many times until it gave way from the hinges and fell into Hope's room with a crash. Hope's eyes were wide, and she had covered her sensitive ears. As soon as he saw her, he enveloped her in a bear hug. He nearly crushed her to him. They kissed like they had been separated for years.

"I can't be away from you, ever." Typhon stared into her eyes. Her response was to grab his cheeks and pull him to her lips. "We have to find Donovan and my sister and get out of here." Hope nodded.

He took her by the hand and led her back to his room, strapped on his weapons and armor and handed her a small shoulder bag.

"What's in here?" Hope asked.

"Healing supplies. You worry about yourself. I'll be fine. If I get hurt you know what happens, so take care of yourself."

"Gotcha."

The pair made their way out of the bedrooms and down the hallway to the teleportation pad. They went down to the next floor.

"I have no idea where Phaedra would be." Typhon said.

"She should be in a bedroom suite with no windows. That's how my father treats his prisoners."

They looked carefully and found a row of windowless rooms. Typhon inspected the main door's hinges. The door flew open. Typhon put his hand up to stop it.

Brother saw sister and they blurted out each other's names.

"Lance."

"Hope."

"What are you doing here?"

Hope peered past him and saw a girl with the same color hair as Typhon. She looked young and afraid.

"I've come to..." she saw her brother breathe deep, "what?"

Lance's eyes took on a red hue. He shut them tight for a second.

"I'm going to bite one of you."

"The hell you are!" Typhon stepped in front of Hope, weapon drawn. Hope backed up.

Lance cackled. He ripped his tunic open. "Take your best shot, St. James!"

Typhon landed what would be a vicious blow to his neck. The sword shattered into pieces. Lance reached out and snatched Typhon by the neck and began to squeeze.

"You will never be a match for me, St. James. I will kill you slowly and make you my fucking monkey," he sneered.

"No!" Hope cried out, as she choked, "Here, feed on me, if you kill him, you kill me."

Lance dropped Typhon in a thud. Typhon gasped and held his throat. Lance hovered over Hope's neck. He wrapped her in his arms and whispered, "We're not even related. Your mother and father aren't mine," He looked into her eyes, "Come with me, be mine, beautiful. You will enjoy it."

Hope shook her head. "That doesn't work on me."

Lance snarled. Then, he howled and let go of her. Hope saw Phaedra behind him. She had fistfuls of his hair.

"Run, now. Both of you. I'll be fine." Phaedra commanded.

Lance turned on Phaedra. He grabbed her in his arms and bit down on her neck like a savage. She fainted.

Hope pulled Typhon up to his feet. "He'll be stronger in a few minutes. We need to regroup and figure out what to do."

They ran to the teleportation pad. Typhon watched in misery as his baby sister was carried into the room by a monster.

"I'm going to kill him in the most heinous way you can kill a vampire."

Hope hugged him. She could feel his anger, desperation, and sadness.

"Let's go find Donovan. Maybe together we can rescue her."

They hadn't paid attention to the floor they were going to. The teleportation ended with the pair in the throne room. Tobias, Illyanna, Donovan and about two dozen guards looked at them.

"Oh shit." Typhon whispered.

Chapter Eighteen

♥

"Welcome, my children," Tobias clapped his hands together and stood up from his throne. Seated next to him, his raven-haired, pale Queen Skyla and both Donovan and Illyanna stood next to her.

Typhon looked at Hope. Fear tore through his mind.

"Hi, Father. We didn't mean to interrupt anything." Hope blurted out.

"Come here, Typhon." Tobias commanded.

Typhon walked over to the King and stopped at the foot of the dais, where he once landed on the floor. He took a knee and bowed his head respectfully.

"Hope. Now you." Tobias beckoned. She obeyed and dipped into a curtsy in front of him, head bowed.

"Donovan, address your needs. Your beloved is here." Tobias sneered. Donovan walked to Hope and gently lifted her chin. She met his eyes. Something had changed. He looked bestial. Typhon turned his head toward them.

"Head down, boy!" Tobias screeched at Typhon. Donovan lifted Hope into his arms. He carried her to a chaise lounge and sat her down.

"It's time, my love, are you ready?" Donovan asked Hope. Her brow furrowed. She moved her head to the side and showed him her neck and shoulder. He bit down on her neck. She winced, but it didn't hurt. Her toes curled under, and she ran her hands into his hair and held him to her. Her blood ran in trickles and stained her dress. Donovan was not careful. He drank from her until he felt her body close to death. He lifted his mouth from her and took a long look at her. Tobias turned Typhon's face toward the couple. Typhon's heart sank. Donovan untied his pants and pressed her skirt up. Typhon jumped up, but Tobias was stronger and held him and made him watch. Donovan hovered over Hope and bit his wrist and pushed it into Hope's mouth. His blood drained into her. Her eyes fluttered open. She swallowed a mouthful and coughed as she did, she felt their bodies intertwine. He pressed his wrist into her mouth and made love to her until she was overcome with passion. Donovan felt it the moment she was bonded to him as a vampire. It overwhelmed them both. Typhon shut his eyes and turned his head away.

"Now this is a party! Wouldn't you agree, family?" Tobias laughed with glee. Tobias snapped and servers came out with blood wine, fine cheese, bread and jams.

"You're insane!" Typhon screamed, "You're all maniacal! Every one of you. If it's the last thing I do, I'll kill the lot of you!"

The Rosedale family and kin all laughed. Tobias let him go.

"Look behind you." Tobias smiled.

Hope stood naked before him. She was radiant. Typhon shot a glare at Donovan. "What have you done to her, Darkblades?"

"Made her the female alpha of our pack." Donovan replied.

"Wha..." Hope took his face into her hands and kissed him so hard, that her newborn fangs nicked him, and he bled. She sucked on his wound. Then, she surprised him and kicked his legs out from beneath him. They landed right in front of the dais, and she climbed atop him.

"I will get to love you forever, Typhon." She said and then ripped his tunic aside and bit him like a savage. He tried to push her off, but Donovan assisted her to keep her on him.

"Hope, please, no. Don't do this to me." Typhon pleaded. She made quick work of him. Then, she shredded his pants. She rode him, ground her hips into his. Typhon tried not to succumb to her. He held onto his humanity with all he had. He felt his consciousness slip away. His eyes shut against his will. Typhon drifted for what seemed forever. Suddenly, he bolted awake. Her slender fingers were in his mouth covered in blood. He instinctively knew he had to take the sustenance offered or die. Typhon let the blood drip into his mouth and swallowed. He felt the exquisite bond between him, Hope, and Donovan. Typhon wanted so much to turn Hope beneath him and take her like a man should, but he couldn't move. Their lovemaking surpassed everything he'd ever dreamed. She was a damn Goddess. *His* Goddess.

"*Our* Goddess." Donovan said aloud. He smiled at Typhon.

Chapter Nineteen

♥

Two days later the trio had moved in a new bedroom prepared for them. Hope had woken up during the night. She tried to sneak over Typhon's body to leave the bed. She lightly padded across the soft carpet and headed to the bath. Hope wanted to wash up. She rounded the corner to see Donovan's form hovered over a young woman. Hope's keen senses smelled the girl's blood. She watched him feed until she was lifeless in his arms. He laid her on the floor, then turned to Hope.

"Come to me, my love," he beckoned, and held his arms out. She ran into his embrace. Donovan hugged her tightly, his face buried in her neck and platinum hair. He could smell her blood. She still had innocent blood! He was instantly sore in the crotch and shifted uncomfortably.

She pulled away. "What's wrong, Donovan?" Then, she saw his face. Red eyes met hers. She was held captive for a brief second. He went to his knees in front of her. He pushed up her dress, and his tongue met her core. Hope's head lulled back. His assault on her was so soft it nearly tickled. She held his hair and pressed him to her. Donovan lifted and pulled her down to the floor. He loosened his pants. He pulled her body to meet his. He leaned down, they kissed deeply as he began to move inside her. He immediately felt her innocence once more. Donovan felt his need build. He was slipping. Hope's body responded to his. She tightened around him. His eyes glowed. Donovan saw her pulse. He dipped down and bit into her. His need for her innocence was too much. His soulmate was so perfect. He wanted to envelope her. Hope's body shuddered and settled down. She clung to him.

Typhon woke up and felt Hope was in danger. He rushed around the chamber as he searched for her or Donovan. He stopped short when he saw them together. Typhon realized Donovan was killing her. Typhon ran in and grabbed Donovan off her. Donovan roared and swung at Typhon. Typhon ducked away. Donovan's eyes glowed.

"Stop, Donovan. You nearly killed her."

Donovan swiped at Typhon's face with his claws. "You're just angry because she loves me more. It's me she wants, not you."

Typhon hauled off and knocked the taste out of Donovan. Donovan careened backward and fell awkwardly into the bath. Typhon jumped in and beat him with another heavy fist to the eye. Donovan turned back to Typhon and hissed with bared fangs.

"Did you just fucking hiss at me like a damn cat?" Typhon laughed. "Calm the hell down, Meow-Man."

"I'll kill you!" Donovan screeched.

At that, the door opened. Mahri Rosedale showed up with a naked female with a bag over her head and her wrists bound to a bar. Both men abruptly stopped fighting and stared at a naked Mahri, then at the girl, then back at Mahri. "Brother, Donovan, come. I've got this lovely morsel for you. As for you, Typhon, don't lay another finger on the new favored son of the King."

Typhon sneered at her. "Shut your whore mouth."

Donovan climbed out of the bath. He walked up and took a long sniff of the girl's body. Typhon watched as Donovan was immediately turned on. Donovan tugged the bag off her head. Typhon's blood froze. *Phaedra.*

"No. Leave her alone, Donovan. That's my sister."

Phaedra's eyes met Typhon's. They were sad.

"We thought it was fitting. Phaedra here won't play nice with our brother Lance." Mahri cooed, her voice dripping with barely hidden cynicism.

Donovan looked over at Typhon, "You'd better rescue Hope."

Mahri took Phaedra and Donovan followed. The door shut behind them.

Mahri stood Phaedra by the bed. "Now watch what you're in for." Mahri started to stroke Donovan until he was fully aroused. Phaedra's eyes were wide.

Donovan walked to Phaedra. He smelled her purity. It brought forth his beast. Mahri smiled at Donovan and left them alone.

Phaedra bravely looked at him in his ruby eyes. Donovan's mouth ached. He wanted to fill it with her blood. Donovan drew strength. Her scent captivated him. "Kid, get out of here. *Go* before I seriously hurt you."

Phaedra's eyes crinkled, "You don't want me after all?"

"I can't do that to Typhon. Now get."

She laid her cheek on his cheek as a little hug. Donovan groaned. She ran for the door and disappeared.

Typhon burst out of the bathroom. He saw Donovan who stood there aroused and alone. "Where's my sister?" he demanded.

"I let her go."

"You better never ever put a finger on her, or I will..."

Donovan crushed his lips on Typhon's. He cut into Typhon's lips.
Typhon tried to back away, but Donovan's strength had grown immensely. "You want some of me, huh, St. James? You've been pissed
at me since day one. Now let's see you try and get yours." Donovan
shoved Typhon down on the bed. Typhon opened his mouth to speak.
Donovan stuck his tongue inside and pressed Typhon into the bed.
A few seconds later Donovan positioned himself just right. Typhon
fought against Donovan to no avail. Donovan smirked down into
Typhon's face and pressed his way inside Typhon so fast and so hard
Typhon jerked and sputtered. Donovan was not kind. He took Typhon rough. He punished him.

Phaedra snuck through the halls. She knew to be caught naked
would be dangerous. She found her room and pressed against the door
as she tried the doorknob. Nothing. She tried to force it open several
times. A familiar voice startled her from behind.

"Hi Phaedra. You look beautiful in that outfit. Something wrong
with your door?"

She turned around as her heart sank. Lance was nose-to-nose with
her. She startled and her mouth fell open slightly. At the same height,
they were looking into each other's eyes. He touched her bottom
lip with his tongue. Phaedra sucked in a breath. He snaked his arm
around her waist. His tongue darted out and found the space between
her lips. He touched her tongue with his. His other hand pressed
her door open. He gently walked her backward, never letting go. He
pushed her up against the nearby wall. She was trapped.

"I have a present for you, Phaedra."

He let her go. She walked over to the closet and started getting
clothes. "Leave it." He commanded. She dropped the clothes. "Come
here, sit."

She sat before him. "What did you get me?"

"Spread your legs." He pushed them apart. She began to wriggle away. He put a hand on each thigh. "Stay very still." He pushed her back on the bed. He spread her legs wide. Phaedra trembled in fear. Lance smiled. He went between her milk-white thighs and was inches away from her womanhood. He spread open her lips. He found her button and stroked it until it swelled and became pronounced. Phaedra protested so many times that Lance looked at her angrily which shut her up.

Once he felt she was ready he opened a small box and took a piercing needle out. "This may sting. It will get better." He pierced her and followed up with a golden ring with a diamond. Phaedra swallowed her tears. Lance gently licked her there to clean the blood away. When he tasted it, his senses soared. Phaedra squirmed as he tasted her. Lance leaned up and handed her a potion of health. "Drink this, darling. Feel better." She drank it down and immediately all her pain stopped. Lance smiled. "Now come." He walked her over to her full-length mirror. She saw her reflection. He spread her open so she could see the beautiful piercing he had given her.

"That's expensive. Why?"

"You haven't figured it out yet have you? You're mine. You will come to see that."

Phaedra looked down. Lance lifted her chin. Their noses touched. He smiled. Then, without warning he quickly pressed his lips to hers. She froze. He didn't press his luck. Phaedra shifted uncomfortably.

Lance noticed. "What's wrong?"

"Nothing." she said softly. She walked away and then stopped abruptly. "What did you do?"

Lance looked confused. "What do you mean?"

"My jewel is...it..."

His face broke into a huge smile. "Feel tingly, maybe good, doesn't it? That's what it's for." He walked over to her, took her hand, and used her index finger to show her to stroke herself. He watched her reaction carefully. First, embarrassment, then she felt pleasure, and finally she collapsed into his arms shaking. "Oh, my Phaedra, you are so beautiful."

"And you...are completely evil." She laughed breathlessly.

"No. *This* is evil." He dropped her onto the bed and put his tongue to the jewel in full motion with every intention of pleasing her. He held her still with strong arms. Phaedra jerked and struggled to get away and then half sat up and came in his mouth. He drank her down. Lance stopped his torture. She watched him leave. She curled up in a ball. A few minutes later, her fingers found their way to the jewel once again.

Typhon was getting beaten on, smacked around, and finally lost consciousness. Donovan's beast was alive and kicking. He smelled virgin essence everywhere. It was like spring flowers in May. He tore out of the room and followed the scent. He came to a door and pressed it open and found Phaedra drifting off to sleep. He yanked the blanket off her. Her scent wafted through the air, and he was painfully engorged. Her eyes opened. He pounced on her. Donovan wasted no time. She wouldn't get away. He guided himself inside of her tiny frame and slammed his hips into hers. Her mouth fell open, and she rose up off the bed. It hurt!

"Oh, my gods, yes!" he cried.

"Please. Donovan, don't hurt me!"

Donovan responded by speeding up his thrusts. His manhood rubbed against her piercing. It slid up and down. Phaedra felt the confusion of pleasure and pain. "Are you on herbs?" he asked her.

"No." she breathed out as she held in her reactions to the increasing pleasure she felt.

"Good."

Their eyes met. She looked shocked. He leaned down and tried to kiss her. She turned her face away. He gave her the lopsided grin. He began to press deeply inside her and pull almost all the way out and then bury himself again.

Phaedra felt a groan escape. He was so deep inside her. Something odd was happening. Donovan pressed inside and moved deeper and deeper. Phaedra's mouth fell open and she clawed his muscular arms. "D...Donovan..."

He could feel her body contracting around him. Donovan was pleased with himself. "How do you want it love?"

"Uh, uh, UHHHH...!" He felt her break loose inside. She kept coming over and over. It was driving him crazy. It was time. Donovan leaned to her neck and without warning bit into her delicate skin. He felt her come again. She was magnificent. A perfect mate for a Dread Vampire. Donovan drank lightly trying only to feed, not get blood drunk. Her blood was spicy. It filled him with warmth. He felt his control give way. He slammed into her and spilled his seed deep within her. He rolled off her.

"Do you have any mystique herbs here?"

Phaedra eyed him warily. "Yes. Why?"

"I want you to take them. *Now.*"

"I, uh..." their eyes met. She got up and pulled some herbs from a small bottle and ate them with some water. "You want me to..."

"Yes."

"I'm very young."

"I know. We will have a big family."

Chapter Twenty

♥

Mahri walked by the trio's room and thought about the handsome Donovan. She was so turned on that she stopped by. She found Typhon knocked out and the King's daughter Hope near death from blood loss in the bathroom. Donovan was missing. She gazed disdainfully at Hope. *Everyone wants a piece of you. You're not so special, can't even hold onto your negative energy to stay a vampire, can you?* Mahri nudged Hope's lifeless body with her foot. She noticed that Hope was healing on her own without vampire traits.

"What are you doing?" Typhon demanded behind her.

"I was coming to visit you three, but something is amiss. Where's Donovan?"

Typhon stared at her, hard. "No, you're here to screw with us. What is your intention, Mahri?"

"Soooo paranoid." Mahri grinned and bared her fangs and claws. She sliced at Typhon and cut fresh lines of blood down his chest. Typhon stepped quick to grab her. A flash of bright white light burst throughout the room, and Typhon heard Mahri's muffled scream and flesh rendered and torn. Blood and body pieces splashed across his body. Typhon was blown off his feet. Where Mahri once stood now empty. Typhon succumbed to the light, feeling his life essence drain away.

Hours later, Typhon smelled something grotesque. His nose wrinkled by the assault of death and gore pervading his nostrils. He slowly rose and realized that Mahri was in chunks, splattered all over the walls. Typhon hurried to check for Hope. She stood in the doorway of the bathroom, clutching at her shoulders. Her face was snow colored. Typhon wrapped his arms around her and pulled her close.

"Ty-Typhon, wh-what happened?" her teeth chattered.

"I'm not exactly sure, but Mahri is literally in pieces. Let's go find Donovan and get the hell out of this place."

Typhon could smell Donovan down the hallway. The couple pressed open the door. To Typhon's surprise, Donovan and Phaedra were in bed together. Hope's brows furrowed.

"How dare you, Donovan? Our bond? I thought you loved me you...you..." Hope stalked out the door and away.

Donovan got up immediately and Phaedra looked confused.

"Did you bed my sister?" Typhon asked as he noticed mystique herbs half taken on the bedside table. "Whoa. Phaedra, you did not take those did you?"

"She did. I asked her."

Typhon swung on Donovan and connected so hard to his temple there was an audible pop. Phaedra was in between them in seconds.

"No, Bubby. Stop. I love him."

"He's a predator. Once the virgin wears off, he'll go to someone new."

A flurry of motion passed them both and landed on Donovan as Lance beat the unholiness out of Donovan. Phaedra covered her mouth with her hand. Lance was so strong.

Hope stood in the doorway. She took a small knife and cut a slit in her shoulder, and let her blood flow. Lance dropped Donovan and turned toward Hope.

"What are you doing, sweetling?" Typhon asked.

"Patch up Donovan." She replied.

Lance ran to Hope, picked her up and left the room. Typhon was so confused. His loyalty was split between his two loves and his sister.

Lance didn't quit running until they reached his bed chambers. He put her up against the wall. "Hope, please. No games."

She gathered her hair away and bared her neck to him. "No games, Lance."

He put her cheeks in his hands. Their eyes locked. "Just relax and let me please you tonight." He slowly leaned in, expecting her to turn away, but she didn't, and he brushed her lips with his. When he probed to slide his tongue between her lips, her eyes closed and she opened to him. Their kiss became desperate and hot.

Her hands held him, pulled at his leather coat. *Wait. Leather waistcoat?* She pulled back so quick; they were both panting. "The only one I know who wears leather like this is..."

She saw a slow, menacing grin spread across Lance's face. The illusion faded. King Tobias in all his glory held her in his arms. "Very observant, my dear. Now, ask yourself, did you want Lance or me?"

She stammered. Hope realized if she said Lance, he was still the King. She was stuck for any answers.

His index finger lifted her chin, and eyes to meet his. She had heard things about his prowess, skill, and how memorable it was. Her eyes dilated. He took note.

Then it dawned on her that Tobias, not Lance, told her that her parents weren't her real parents. Who was this King she served? She shuddered. Her head swam with thoughts. Then, she felt his breath

across her lips. Her eyes flicked forward. Their lips met. She gasped
into his mouth. She was kissing the *King*. He coaxed her backward
until she was up against the wall. He pressed his entire body against
hers. *My, he is built, everywhere.* She felt tiny against him. He hoisted
her up to match his height. Then, she felt it. So long and sleek, so hard.
She moaned. His tongue moved down her neck to her shoulder. He
kissed her, and she felt a small sting. Then, something so overwhelm-
ing came over her she wriggled and pressed her own hips into his. She
realized he was feeding. It felt exquisite. She came several times. Hope
had such devastating orgasms tears fell. Her body wanted Tobias. She
would die without his touch. *What was this sudden need for him?* Her
thoughts left her as she began to come for him repeatedly. Then, she
felt it. He entered her. She howled with pleasure. He was oh so damn
huge, long, *perfect.* He took her own fingers and showed her how to
rub herself during lovemaking. She cried so many tears of pleasure.
Her body moved in time with his. He made her his over and over. Her
moans became his name. He exploded seed inside her. He came so hard
that he trembled when he was finished.

"Oh, my gods, my King, I..."

"Tobias."

She eyed him carefully, "Tobias. I have never. I mean I didn't know
it could be like...ooooh. Something's happening." She clung to him.

Tobias, who was still inside her, felt her clench. His dark side, his
hidden secret, was responding to her. Confusion and something else
were growing in his gut. *Bloody Hells, I want her again.* He realized
he couldn't hold his secret in a moment longer. Thank the gods her
eyes were closed and she was distracted. He started to move inside
her again. A bright yellow-white light burst from her and he felt
warmth, love, and a fierce attraction to it. He felt her press against
him. Her body was ready for him again. He held onto her tight. Tobias

tried to concentrate on pleasing her, but he was transforming. He felt the darkness radiating and pulsating, growing. The familiar waves of dizziness caught him. He heard her and felt her come. He cried out as the transformation completed itself. Tobias King was gone. In his place stood Melchior, God of Evil. His evil side now truly out, was getting off on corrupting such a pure creature.

He turned her around and entered her in the backside. Melchior wanted her ruined in all ways. Hope, now shining with brilliant bright light, was hurting his eyes, but he felt so perfect inside her.

Hope felt him invade her backside. The new sensations sent her reeling. She felt feelings of love growing. Tobias shuddered and came again. She was breathless, but she turned around and when she did her now angelic face fell.

"Melchior?! I, who, what is going on?"

"I should ask you the same. *Hope.*" He sneered her name. She shook her head. He marched her to the mirror. The God of Elemental Evil stood behind her. She now glowed with white light, had the gossamer wings of a Fae, and was taller than she was as an Elf.

"I, I don't know what I am." Hope said honestly and looked at Melchior in the mirror.

"You are a descendant of the race of Elves that bred with the Fae at the beginning of this world. You're a being of purity, light, and love. Exactly the *opposite* of me."

She turned around and looked at Melchior. "I won't tell anyone. I don't know why we had this happen. Do you? I have never looked like this."

"Your secret is safe. I just can't decide if I want to kill you or take you to bed again."

"This is wrong. We're complete opposites. This has to mean something. I can't just walk myself out of this room looking like some Faery Princess."

They stood there together for a moment and a sparkling light entered the room. Tatiana, the Goddess of Love, dressed in a beautiful pink lace dress, her hair up and fastened with roses, came into existence.

"What do *you* want?" Melchior asked, rolling his eyes.

Tatiana bowed to both of them. "My Lord of Evil, Lady of Purity, you two are a balancing act for each other. It is Fate. You will either kill each other or balance the energies your God-Selves produce. Which will it be? Time will tell. You are like a sword to a scabbard. There is no denying one another. Don't try." Tatiana burst into sparkles and dissipated.

"Well, it won't be me killing you." Hope said.

Melchior laughed. "Can I corrupt the Lady of Purity enough to have her commit murder?"

"Tobias! No!" she laughed.

His countenance dropped. "I wasn't kidding." He said gravely. He stepped towards her with an ominous look in his black eyes. She stepped back. He walked her backwards till she fell over the bed backwards. Hope panicked. "Spread your legs, Lady." She didn't listen to him so he moved between her knees and shoved her thighs apart. Hope squeaked. He began licking and sucking on her as he held her still. His forked tongue delighted her. He stuck it inside of her and wiggled it and she came hard. He tasted her returned purity and it drove him wild. Then, he fed from her inner thigh. She bucked and arched off the bed. Melchior felt the need to harm her. He went to his dresser and came back. Like Phaedra, he pierced Hope the same way. Melchior wasn't gentle to Hope. He finished with the piercing and licked it and played with it with his tongue. Much to his dismay, Hope loved it.

"You're fucking evil. You like it." Melchior said.

Breathless, she sat up, "Take me, Melchior."

His jaw hit the floor, but he didn't have to be told twice. He shoved himself inside her and the couple couldn't keep their hands off one another for two days straight.

The early morning of the third day Hope had fallen asleep in his luxurious bed. Melchior stared at her all night. He couldn't stand her light, her goodness. He wanted her, needed her to be sure, but he wanted to corrupt her from the inside out. Like some possessed animal, Melchior hovered over her with a serrated dagger ready to end her. The dagger could kill Gods. He held it aloft to strike and then heard it. A heartbeat. No, not Hope's. Not his. Her *child's*. He lowered the dagger immediately and put his hand splayed on her belly and concentrated. *His child*. Melchior staggered back. Shock and awe blew his mind. He put the dagger back in his belt. She was going to give birth to a natural Deity. Melchior began planning for his child's arrival. No one would ever touch Hope again but him.

Chapter Twenty-Two

♥

Outside the door of "Lance's" bedchambers Phaedra and the other two men stood perplexed by what they heard.

"Um, that's the damn King in there with our woman." Typhon stated, grimly.

"Yeah. We're not top dog now. I've heard about his skill with women." Donovan looked nonplussed.

Phaedra growled low. "Donovan, do you not care for me?"

"Yes, but that's my soulmate in there. I'm sorry. We three have a bond you don't understand, at least we did," he said as he looked at the door.

They hid as the door opened. A tall, cloaked figure walked out of the room and shut the door. The figure disappeared on the teleportation pad. The trio ran to the door and Phaedra made quick work to unlock it. Her unbeknown talent was a shock to Typhon.

"We'll talk about this later, Phaedra," Typhon whispered. She smiled to herself. They came into the room to find Hope tied up on the bed.

"Donovan? Typhon? You're both here. Please let me up." Hope pleaded.

Typhon undid her straps. She sat up on the bed. When she stretched out a pair of beautiful glimmering wings spread out behind her. She held a child-like appearance and seemed even more youthful than Elven magic could grace her with. Donovan and Typhon both just stared agape. She was so beautiful she outmatched a nymph, a Goddess.

"Why are you staring at me?"

"You, you're new." Typhon said.

Donovan gingerly reached out to touch her, when his fingers touched her cheek, he felt the magic radiating from her. It made the vampiric side in him go crazy. He turned from her and put his hands over his face as his full fangs extended and he felt his beast pushing out of his soul. Typhon leaned down and placed a light kiss on her lips. He gasped as his body reacted like a school boy getting his first blow job. "You're a holy fire, Hope. I don't know how, but somehow you blew past beautiful and made it to Goddess."

Donovan paced outside in the hall. He needed blood or sex or to kill something. What was wrong with him that he couldn't touch his own beloved? Donovan's anger rose until he was enraged. She belonged to him. *This was the King's fault. What the hell did he do to her? I will have my love back if I have to murder the King of Rosedale. Nothing else matters to me but my two soulmates.*

Donovan shook his dark thoughts away. He walked back to the bedroom and saw Typhon place a kiss on Hope's soft pink lips. Donovan snarled and lunged at Typhon in hot jealousy. Hope jumped back. She put Phaedra behind her. The two men fought until Typhon was a scratched and blood covered mess. Typhon lost consciousness. When Donovan saw her, standing there Fae wings spread her beauty outshining all things he dropped to his knees. "I don't know what's wrong with me." He moaned to her.

Then, Donovan felt his beast come alive again. He licked his lips. He ran to Hope. "I need you." He begged.

She reached up to his face. "I love you." She gently kissed him. It burned him, but he barely felt the pain. Hope went to Typhon. She leaned down and looked at Donovan sadly. "What did you do to him?"

"I beat him down. I was just so angry."

"He loves you, like I do, you must learn to control yourself." Hope's lips turned down for a second. She could feel Donovan's shame. *What a mess. How do I control these mortals? Wait, did I just use the word "mortals?" These are my beloveds.* Hope looked down and shook her head to stop the odd stream of thoughts.

Phaedra sniffed the air. "The King is coming."

Donovan took Phaedra's hand and pulled her behind a floor-length tapestry. He pressed his finger to her lips. She nodded.

His footfalls rounded the corner and Tobias stood before her. No trace of Melchior was left. "Who has been in here? I smell blood."

Hope put her hands up toward him. "Don't get angry. They tried to save me, but got into a fight. Typhon is beat up. Donovan fled in shame."

He cracked a smile. Tobias reached out and snagged her forearm and yanked her to him. "*Don't. Lie. To. Me.* Where are Donovan and Phaedra? Either you tell me and they live, or I find out and they suffer."

Donovan came out of the tapestry. He put Phaedra behind him. "My King. I am here." Donovan took a knee.

"Excellent. I have decided. You will marry Miss St. James tomorrow. I will see to everything."

Phaedra's countenance turned from shock to anger. "I'd rather marry Lance."

Tobias laughed so hard he took a step backward to steady himself. He looked right into her eyes and in a voice dripping with hatred, "I was Lance, you ignorant bitch."

Phaedra's face drained of color. She couldn't feel her legs and collapsed into Donovan's arms. Donovan caught her and held her close. He looked at Hope, then at the King.

"Well, go on. Leave. Both of you." Tobias commanded.

Hope turned to Tobias. "What about Typhon?"

"I'll have him taken to the infirmary. You come with me."

"But..." Hope protested.

"Shut it!" Tobias roared.

"You shut it, Tobias! I won't allow you to talk to me that way, *mortal*!" the hate-filled words surprised her as they left her lips.

Tobias raised a fist to her. "Woman, Fae, whatever the hells you are, don't make me. I will."

She erupted in bright searing light and took a step toward him. Tobias screeched and covered his eyes and felt the skin on his face, outer arms and hands start to bubble, pop, and sizzle. The pain was excruciating. She took another step forward. He walked backwards.

"Hope, stop. I'm dying."

"Don't you ever raise your hand to me again. I will kill you."

The bright light faded. Tobias was blinded for several minutes and felt his fast healing take over. It offered sweet relief. When he blinked and saw her standing before him, he could barely contain himself. He licked his lips. Her power had disintegrated her clothing, the pins in her hair. She stood before him in glory and natural beauty. It was almost more than he could bear. His eyes fell on her piercing. It was peeking out showing that she was swollen. Tobias groaned.

"Hope, you belong to me. You are the one I have waited all my long life for. Stay with me. I need you." He began to shake visibly.

She ran her fingers down his cheek. Traced his lips. She walked to him and placed a gentle kiss on his mouth. He groaned into her mouth. He slid his hand between their bodies, seeking her piercing. When he found it, he realized she was ready for him. He teased her in circles until she was panting in pleasure.

"Hope..." he leaned back and looked into her blue eyes, "Melchior will never admit this, but I have to. I, we, love you. We need you in our lives. There is no one else. You are the one."

"Tobias, hush, you are incapable of love. Melchior especially."

Tobias picked her straight up and carried her to the nearest wall and unlaced his pants. He entered her gently, not wanting to hurt his child. They made love, as he kissed her the entire time.

"Oh, Tobias, why can't you be like this always? Mmmm..."

"I will be for the next year. You have that to look forward to."

"What? Why a year?"

Then, she met his eyes and something turned him on greatly and he moaned loudly and called her name and came so hard she felt it deep inside. She made a face, confused.

He kissed her long and hard. "In a year, my love, something special will happen."

"Wha..." then it dawned on her, "Oh my gods, I'm expecting." She ran a hand over her stomach. She looked up at him with wonder in her eyes.

"*My* child. *Our* child. A full Deity." Tobias said proudly.

"Oh, my gods, you knew...Tobias, I can't. I love Typhon and Donovan."

"It's Fate, love. There's nothing to be done now. You are a daughter of Gods and Goddesses. You deserve so much more than two measly mortals." Melchior burst out before her.

Her eyes drank him in. His dark features, long silky black hair, black eyes. Skin-tight pants and chiseled arms, back and chest. She reached out and touched his arms with her hands, then traced across his chest. A little gasp escaped her lips and she bit his nipple and sucked on it. He held her there and laid back on the bed with her on top and let her explore his body. She made her way down him, trailing hot kisses in her wake. She put her soft lips around him and took him into her mouth and he grew so hard it hurt.

Typhon woke up to the sounds of...*what the hell is that noise?* He staggered around the corner to see his beautiful woman Elf going down on someone, and really giving it to him. He should've been pissed, but something turned him on.

"Oh, my gods, Hope. You're so damn hot." Typhon groaned.

Melchior beckoned Typhon over to the bed. He walked over. Melchior yanked the laces out of Typhon's pants. He pulled Typhon close and closed his mouth around his manhood and sucked so hard Typhon thought the back of his hips would cave in. Typhon could barely stand it. He surrendered to this stranger. Hope was so turned on that she got on top of Melchior and rode him while he pleasured Typhon. Typhon tried to pull away, even protested aloud that he was getting close. Melchior just pressed him inside his mouth further.

"Oh my God! *Fuck!*" Typhon jerked and came in torrents in this stranger's mouth. To his delight the stranger swallowed. Typhon gently lifted Hope off of the stranger and sat her on the man's face. Melchior immediately went to work on her piercing and Hope pressed herself down into his mouth. Typhon entered Melchior and returned the favor. He quickly jacked off Melchior as he fucked him. All three began to moan in sync. The dark light of Melchior started encircling the room and Hope's white light began joining it until the energies made a flow that went through and around everyone and everything.

They all came at the same moment. The room was electric. They all fell on the bed together basking in the unity.

"What was that?!" Typhon asked.

"Awesome." Sighed Hope.

"A Bond that surpassed mortal ones." Melchior explained.

"What? How?" Typhon asked confused.

Melchior sat up and looked at Typhon. He touched his forehead. "Come out." A black energy bolt hit Typhon's head. Typhon staggered, grabbing his head. He fell to his knees. Hope sprang up to run to him. She was at his side in a second holding onto him.

"What did you do?" she hissed at Melchior.

"You'll see. You'll thank me."

"Baby, it's ok. I'm here." Hope said softly. Typhon contorted and shifted uncomfortably. Rending flesh and breaking bones pervaded the air. Hope covered her mouth in horror. Typhon grew to unbelievable size and stature. He resembled someone she could barely recall. "Who are you?" Hope asked him.

From under the figure's cloak, he simply said, "Pax."

Chapter
Twenty-Three

♥

Donovan carried Phaedra back to his bedroom. He laid her out on the bed while he paced nervously. Eventually, she woke up.

"Donovan, we have to get everyone out of here. I do not want to marry you. No offense."

"None taken. I just want to get them out of his clutches. He's pure evil."

"He has to stop having sex eventually." She shrugged.

"Maybe, or maybe he has a super cock?" Donovan ground out. Phaedra laughed in spite of the situation.

Night fell and both Phaedra and Donovan snuck down the hall without sound. Outside the door, they heard Typhon speaking in hushed tones. Phaedra unlocked the door again.

Donovan whispered, "Princess Breaking and Entering." Phaedra smiled.

They walked in the door. Both Typhon and Hope stood up defensively.

"Phaedra, you, okay?"

"Yes, brother. Donovan took care of me." Typhon gave Donovan the stink eye.

"What?! I made sure she was safe." Donovan pleaded.

"Let's get out of here." Hope said, "I know a way out." She led them down the back way and down old musty staircases. It was a long journey down several floors, but they saw no one on the way. Once they reached the bottom floor of the palace, it was stones for flooring and damp. They snuck out of a back door. The group ran for the nearest stables when they left the palace grounds.

"Rosedale will find us eventually. I say we continue north into the hills and then to the Kingdom of Surilla. I have heard that their king is welcoming to visitors." Typhon said.

"Good idea." Hope responded. Everyone began packing up supplies and Phaedra brought extra horses and loaded them down for a long journey. Typhon looked at Hope with a worried look. "We need to put a cloak on you or something. Just one look at you and men will fall all over themselves trying to capture you." Hope, now wearing a ridiculously oversized cloak, was helped onto a horse and Typhon climbed in the saddle behind her. Donovan frowned but swung up in the saddle of his war horse. Phaedra noticed Donovan's chagrin with a side-eyed glance. They rode straight north into deeper woods, but Typhon directed them all onto a hidden path. Donovan noticed how intelligent Typhon was in the natural setting. As they rode, Hope nestled into Typhon's strong broad chest. His arm encircled her, and she felt safe.

A few hours later they cleared the forest and saw hills stretching out for what seemed eternity. It was the beautiful grassy hills of Terrian, human territory. Wild berries and wheat grew everywhere and no roads were to be found. They ventured forth and crossed up and down hills for miles. A brigade of human soldiers on horseback stopped them. They were encircled and swords were held out by every man.

The man in full plate spoke, "What business have you here in Terrian?"

"We're passing through to Surilla. Nothing more." Typhon answered.

"That cloaked figure. Stranger, let down your hood."

The group all looked at Hope. She let down her hood and some gasps went up in the unit of men when they saw how otherworldly she looked. Hope was frightened.

"Come with us. The King of Terrian will want to see you."

"But why?" Donovan asked. Typhon slapped him on the chest.

"To decide your fate."

Hope looked at Donovan and Typhon, her eyes were wide with fear.

They rode in the center of the circle for over three hours to the north-west. The company came to a large city, walled in stone, with a gothic appeal. They were taken immediately to the castle and before the king. When the king arrived, he too was wearing an ankle-length cloak with his hood up. He walked straight up to Hope.

"So, this is the woman you sent word about. Let's have a look." He pulled back her hood. When he saw her face, he quickly undid her cloak brooch and the cloak fell to her feet. Hope looked down and covered her face with her hands.

The cloaked king lifted her chin with a finger. "Look at your King. What is your name?"

"Hope. Rosedale."

"Now, guards, escort the rest of her party to rooms. I wish to speak with Hope alone. Tonight, we shall feast."

"You don't get to touch her, or speak with her without us present!" Donovan yelled.

A guard struck out to hit him in the mouth. Donovan clawed him across the knuckles, then across the face.

"Control that animal!" the king shouted.

Donovan was coming in to kill the guard when chanting started and chains and shackles encased his hands behind his back and feet together and he hissed and fell to the floor. Typhon's eyes widened in surprise. Hope's eyes filled with tears. Phaedra turned her face away. She couldn't bear to watch Donovan taken captive.

The guards disarmed the other party members. They drug Donovan to a holding cell. They showed the others to rooms. Hope stood there in front of the king feeling naked and vulnerable. He put her hand in his.

"I am going to lay it on the line. You have a choice to make. You hold the key to your friends' destiny. Accept my offer and they go free, deny me and they suffer while you watch."

Her face dropped. Her mouth gaped. Hope's eyes filled with fury. She started to cast a spell, and he grabbed her hands. "You are a bastard! I was told you were welcoming. It was lies."

"Come, Lady. I wish to talk to you, in private." She walked with him. Her gut was screeching at her to run, attack, do anything but obey, but fear won out. The couple reached a large bedroom that looked more like an apartment. He offered her to sit on the lounger, and he stood before her.

His eyebrow arched. Then he laughed. "I can kill you or them in a moment's notice. Just a mere word. What will it be?"

A shiver ran down her spine, as he lifted her chin again. There was something wholly unsafe and evil in his touch. Something she'd never felt before.

"Stop touching me!" she yelled at him.

He let go. "My terms are that you stay with me in this bedroom for a season and then you and your friends can leave, but I will own you for that entire length of time. Do you understand?"

Her mouth fell open at the ghastly idea. He laughed at her reaction. "No, you cannot own a person."

"Fine, then you forfeit their lives." He turned and stalked toward the door. She ran after him and touched his back.

"No wait. Don't. I-I accept your terms."

He turned to face her. "How cute. Real love. Such weakness." He walked over to a dresser and took out leather handcuffs, a collar, and ankle cuffs. "You will dress in this and nothing else. No one else may see you but me. You listen only to me. Now get dressed. I'll be back in a few minutes."

Hope's tears fell in torrents as she undressed and put the cuffs on her body. She buckled the collar in place and then looked at her reflection in the mirror. She looked like a Fae. Her thoughts were interrupted by the opening of the door.

"You look like a nymph. *My* nymph. Now, go lay on the bed."

Hope didn't at first move so she got a hard smack on her bare ass. She stared up at the cloaked figure. Anger seething, nostrils flaring. She went to the bed and laid down. "Now what, your Highness." She spouted out with venom dripping in her voice.

He yanked her up and turned her over. She yelped as he cracked a cat o' nine across her thighs. "You will address me as 'lord'. Do you understand?"

"Fuck you!" she yelled then cried out as the cat o' nine raked her thighs once more.

"Say: My Lord. Say it."

"NO!" He hit her once on the thighs, once on the ass. The red streaks he left were turning him on.

"Say it, now, just say it and it ends."

"I hate you!" He whipped the cat o' nine across her ass, she cried out again, which just made him harder.

He turned her over and saw her chest heaving from heavy breaths, her large breasts nearly shoved in his face because her hands were behind her back, and her pierced womanhood all for the taking. "You are delicious." He undid his cloak and the shock on her face made him grin widely at her. He was not human at all. He was the Unseelie Prince. He was rumored to be so cruel and merciless that he couldn't keep a mate alive. His skin was almost a gray color, his hair pure white, long, like silken threads. He bore tattoos of odd symbols down both arms. Speaking of his arms they were so brawny and built she couldn't help but stare. That led to his chest. His royal symbol hung around his neck and his rippled six-pack was to die for. No wonder women fell all over him. Then, her gaze dropped lower his chiseled waist and his manhood, fully erect, bigger than Typhon. She was embarrassed. She squeezed her eyes shut. She felt his magic, his energy. He was no longer hiding it from her. Two could play this game. She unfurled her energy of light. Maybe it would burn him like it did Donovan. She looked at him in this battle of wills. His arms were one on either side of her head, his body poised over hers. She knew that he could claim her if he only wanted. She felt the push-pull of the dark and light, the love-hate. He held his position staring at her, into her eyes. She met his eyes. They were glowing blue. She fought with her energy against him, but quickly became tired. She hadn't figured out how to properly channel it yet. He smiled at her.

"I'm winning." He said softly. He laid his body upon hers. His energy surrounded her and she felt exhausted. She looked into his eyes, searching for any sign of what was to come. "Call me 'lord'"

"No." she whispered.

"Stubborn brat!"

His face turned so evil that it scared her. He raised his hand to her. "You will talk respectful to me, or I will beat you. Do you understand me, Seelie?"

She sighed. "Yes."

"Yes what?"

"Yes, you prick."

He backhanded her. She fell over the bed in a whoosh. She felt her cheek swelling.

"Tomorrow, if you say one unkind word to me, I will make sure you pay." His face was dead serious. He turned and left, locking her in. She laid there crying until she fell asleep.

The next evening, she awoke to the sound of the door opening. The prince had returned, but it was still pitch dark in the room and outside.

"Good evening, Seelie." He walked over to her and picked her up under the arms and stood her up next to him. She saw in the dim light his eyes glowing blue. Their energies mingled, waiting to fight for control. She tried to step back but was against the bed. He leaned his face down and placed a soft kiss on her mouth. He saw her beautiful eyes like ice daggers staring into his when he pulled up from the kiss.

She cleared her throat, "Good evening." He smiled at her answer. She was being good.

She looked into his eyes. He leaned down and brushed a kiss over her lips. This time she didn't fight him. He cocked his head to the side and looked at her.

"What do you want from me?"

"An heir."

"What?!"

"Eventually, I will take you every single day, Seelie, until you are pregnant with my heir."

"I don't want to bear your, an Unseelie child."

"It will be half Seelie."

"I'm not..."

"Yes, you are."

"Fine. Whatever. I don't want to leave a child of mine in your hands. You're evil."

"Only from your perspective."

"You need to eat, Seelie."

"Call me Hope."

He pulled her close and kissed her hard, parting her lips with his tongue. She tasted herself in his mouth.

"Sleep for a while. I'll make sure you eat when you wake up. Goodnight." He got up to leave and she softly whispered to him.

"What's your real name?"

He turned back to her. He grinned. "My lord." And walked out the door, locking it behind him. He laughed to himself when he heard her frustrated scream.

Chapter
Twenty-Four

D onovan was chained to the wall both hands and feet like a
beast. His cuffs and chains were magic so he couldn't mist step
out of them. He was starving. It had been two days with no sustenance
and his blood supply was lacking. His head hung, and he drifted in
and out of a strange dream-like state. The door to his cell opened and a
servant walked in. She tip-toed towards his feet and was about to place
a dish of food in front of him when his head flew up. His eyes, red slits,
focused in on her.

"Hey, girl. Please will you help me?" his voice was soft and inviting.

"What do you need, filth?" she sneered.

"I need to feed, could you offer me your wrist, your neck, anything?
I will die if I don't get what I need. It doesn't hurt." His voice sounded
like a song to her ears.

She eyed him carefully. Slowly, she leaned down to him, handed out
her wrist. "There."

He bit into her wrist and she flinched from the pleasure she felt.
Donovan sucked greedily on her, gulping her lifeblood down. She

tried to pull away, but he dug his fangs in deeply. He took more and more. His strength was returning. The girl collapsed in front of him. He let her go. Donovan reveled in the feelings the blood gave as it circulated in his system. He waited. The girl woke up.

"Do you feel weak?" Donovan asked her.

"Yes. I do."

"Go, eat, no wine," he looked into her eyes, "tell no one. Come back to me and let me feed from you daily." The girl blinked and nodded. Donovan was coming up with a plan of escape using this girl even as she walked out the door.

Meanwhile, the prince returned to Hope's room. She looked at him and struggled against her bonds. He wore black leathers and pants with matching black leather boots, all Elven made.

"Don't worry, Seelie, I've come to show you something, not bed you."

"What do you want to show me?"

The prince held out his hand, palm facing her. The Elven gesture of 'hello'. She smiled and held her hand to reciprocate. Their hands met. Time and space shifted around Hope. Her vision of the bedroom apartment faded, and she found herself standing in soft grass, barefoot. A white, diamond encrusted wedding gown touched her ankles. She witnessed her marriage to the dark prince. Her light glowing brightly, his shadow balanced by it. He carried her through the forest path as twinkling purple and green pixies dotted the landscape, hiding beneath mushrooms and behind twisted trees. The scent of fresh herbs and flowers filled Hope's senses. They climbed the stairs to the spire tower. He laid her down on the bed and the scene switched as Hope saw their son. A young Fae Elf with silver hair and bright blue eyes looked directly at Hope. Her heart melted. She had a soul-filled need to reach out to the young boy. When she could no longer stand it and went to stroke his hair, the vision faded, and she realized she had moved her hand away from the prince's.

"I can give you that future." He stated.

"I don't believe you. It's just Fae magic."

"I have a gift for you. It is time."

"Time for what?" She asked, concerned.

"Your training." He walked her to the bed and strapped her face-down to the bed on her knees. "Now relax, Seelie." She heard a drawer open and shut. His footsteps. Then, his warm breath on her ear. "Ready?" He gently pressed a smooth phallus between her legs. "Seelie Fae love jade. Enjoy." He pushed the phallus inside of her and the tingles it produced traveled her entire body.

"Oh!" she exclaimed as his rhythm became steady.

"You are so beautiful, my Seelie mate."

She came at that moment. Shivering, she completely relaxed under his touch.

"Mmm...good. You are pleased." He rubbed her piercing until she was drenched. "Do you want me now, Seelie, because it feels like it." He turned her over and kissed her as he undid his pants. He took off her shackles. He positioned himself over her. She looked seriously afraid. The pain was searing when he entered her but it didn't last. One hard thrust and he buried himself in her. The feeling of them together, the balance, this was too right. She wrapped her legs around his waist and gave herself to him. She couldn't help it. This Unseelie King was an ass but also simply too amazing for words. They slept the night together in the big bed and he was still there the next morning.

Meanwhile, night had fallen on the rest of the group and Phaedra had snuck about looking for the cell Donovan was in. When she found it, she assassinated the guard by slitting his throat. Then, she took his keys and snuck into the cell room.

"Donovan." She hugged him. Donovan bit down on her neck. She swallowed and bit her lip to not cry aloud in pleasure. She wrapped her hand around his head and steadied him to take as much as he needed. His ecstasy in her was always so complete. She leaned back and put her hands on his cheeks and kissed him. Donovan was shocked but realized she had feelings behind it. He bit his own lip and they shared blood. He was so hard for her. His need to turn her, to mate with her permanently was getting stronger every time they had an encounter.

"Let's go, Donovan, before someone notices the guard."

He took her hand and they left together.

"Let's go find Typhon. Then, we'll all rescue Hope." Donovan stated.

"What kind of wine is that?"

"It's Fae wine, my Seelie. Drink deep."

She finished the entire cup. He tries to hide his smile, knowing he added his blood to the wine. Soon, he knew they would be bonded perfectly. Matched for eternity and it would unite the Seelie and Unseelie Courts under his ruling. He would have her produce an heir to continue on this lineage. He had big plans for her. He knew that she was of Godly heritage. Her father, a King of the Seelie Court, bringer of life to Veldar. She had no idea who she was. Her Elven mother had been chosen by the Seelie King to produce heirs since she was a Starseed. Now, his precious carried on that immortal trait. She was meant to be his, not to be wasted on common blooded Elves and Half-breeds. He would stop at nothing to tear the trio apart. Starting with her love for Typhon.

Later that evening, after midnight, the prince returned to Hope's bedside. He had a bottle of wine this time. He shared it with her until she was drunk on his blood and the Unseelie mushrooms that it was made out of, a kind of ecstatic drug. Her eyes were glazed over and dilated. Hope burped and clapped her hand over her mouth. The prince smiled.

"Kiss me," he tilted his head towards her and ran a finger down her cheek. She got close to his lips and to his amusement she stuck out her tongue.

"Nope, and yous can't makes me...You're nots my boss."

"Really?" his brow arched. He left her there. A few minutes later the prince returned with Typhon. Typhon talked to the prince like they were great friends as they walked into the room together. The prince pushed Typhon forward onto his knees in front of Hope. Typhon looked at Hope and smiled for an instant.

"Hope, I've been in a room for..."

"You want him? Show me how bad, Seelie."

Hope's world spun. She was hot, felt giddy, and couldn't form a sentence. The prince whispered something into Typhon's ear. Then, he slowly lifted Hope off the side of the bed into his arms. She shot him a confused look. He faced her toward Typhon. She felt his right-hand cup her breast, and the left found her sensitive folds. She gasped. He kissed her ear, dropped his mouth to her neck and sucked on her skin. Hope squeezed her eyes shut and tried to think of anything but his hot touch. "Now, now, look him in the eyes, Seelie." Typhon's stormy eyes met hers.

Typhon recognized the look of passion in an instant. His soulmate enjoyed the dark one's antics. She tried to hide it, but her flushed cheeks and dilated eyes gave her away. He blinked and looked away. Typhon tried to convince himself that Hope's naked beauty and that damn piercing weren't a bother. It didn't work. He felt himself respond to the sight.

"That's right, Typhon. You can't resist her, can you?" the prince crooned. "She's wet, for me, not you. That doesn't matter, does it?

You're just a Half-breed boy with a useless title trying to play with the men. Now come for me, Seelie." His voice was a purr in her delicate ear. He reinforced the command with a blast of his dark energy so harsh that her body jolted and gave into him. He caught her up against his own body and she turned her face to him and they shared a deep tongued kiss. At that, he bent her over in front of Typhon and took her hard until she was audibly wet and coming repeatedly.

"Say my name, Seelie." He panted.

"Cassian!" she cried to him, as he pounded her from behind.

Typhon watched in disgust. He heard a voice say, "Go get your friends, take this one chance to leave, unless of course, you still want her?"

"Cassian, oh, oh gods, Cassian!" Hope cried aloud as a strange pleasure overtook her.

Typhon shook his head, then got up and left the room. Cassian poured himself into Hope and laid her on the bed afterward. He watched from a scrying mirror as Typhon searched for his sister and Donovan.

Chapter Twenty-Five

♥

P haedra and Donovan had just fought off the last of the guardians of the bedroom area. Donovan looked pained throughout the battle. Phaedra was not very helpful and mostly threw things at the guards. When Phaedra dispatched her last warrior, she turned to Donovan. "You okay?"

"Yes, I..." he crossed the steps between them and in the midst of the blood and gore he pulled her to him and bit down into the nape of her neck. He had barely taken any blood when he heard her moan his name under her breath. Donovan lost it and stuck his hand down her skirt, found her diamond and to his surprise she gently opened herself to him. When he touched the jewel and played with it, she came several times. "You are so fucking beautiful, Phaedra." He moaned against her bloody neck. She answered by coming again. Typhon turned the corner just in time to overhear this. He stopped short and hid. He watched in secret. Typhon felt Donovan's intense pleasure. He wasn't even being touched and he grew enormous with need. Donovan took Phaedra's skirt down and her shirt up and worked on her nipples with his tongue until she arched in his arms. Typhon, as if possessed, could barely contain himself. He rubbed himself through his laces. He was so hard, it hurt. Typhon pulled his pants laces loose and tossed his shirt off and lightning quick took out Donovan with his newfound vampire strength.

Phaedra stood still shocked. Her brother had darted out half naked, almost as if drunk and taken out her almost lover. Then, he turned to Phaedra, and in a second flash had her in his arms and was sucking the blood out of her neck and then she felt it: his fingers. He touched her, *there*. She gasped so loud and struggled against him but he was experienced. He rubbed her expertly, like he loved her.

"No! Brother, don't! What is wrong with you?!" Phaedra pushed against him with all her might, with everything her will could muster. This was *wrong*.

"I WILL FUCKING KILL YOU!"

A flash of movement and Phaedra fell to the floor in a heap onto a bleeding corpse. Her hand steadied her fall inside the torn-out heart cavity.

A roar vibrated her bones jarring her out of her utter disgust. The two men were ripping each other to shreds with teeth and claws. Phaedra only watched until Donovan went for the killing blow and throat grabbed Typhon, even at his height difference.

"NO! Donovan, stop! That's my brother!" She found herself at his waist. She clung to him. Wrapped herself around him, and begged. Donovan's eyes cleared for a brief second. He saw his Phaedra in tears at his side. He tossed his friend across the room like trash.

"Phaedra," Donovan said with tenderness, "let's get out of here." He lifted her up and into his arms and left the room and walked right by Typhon as he bled profusely.

Chapter Twenty-Six

When they got outside, the guards didn't stop them.

"His Highness has allowed for you two to leave. Do not return." The captain said.

When they were far enough away from the castle, Phaedra looked back and then at Donovan. "What now?"

He stopped and sighed. His arms akimbo, he looked worn out. It scared Phaedra. He always seemed so strong. This was the first time he looked almost...and the word rang in their minds...*mortal*. His eyes flicked to hers.

"But, I'm not." Donovan whispered as if his voice were a scream on the quiet breeze.

Phaedra looked confused. "I didn't say anything, Donovan."

The tendril of attraction cemented at that moment in time. He reached out to her and caressed her cheek. She nestled her face into his fingers.

"I love you, Phaedra."

She looked up at him, a brilliant smile on her face. "You do? What about Hope?"

The pained look flashed just long enough for her to see it. Phaedra knew. He would never be over Hope, and that was something she could not live with. She instinctively turned away from him as tears brimmed her eyes.

"Son." It was Tobias Rosedale's voice from behind.

Donovan turned and put Phaedra at his back. Sure enough, Tobias somehow had gotten there in the flesh. "What do you want? If you're here for Hope..."

"I'm here for my son, you. Hope is no more my daughter than Phaedra."

Donovan eyed him suspiciously. "What do you mean?"

"Your mother and I are waiting to talk to you, about many things. Come. The time is drawing near when we will fight side-by-side whether you wish it or not."

"I must go see to my brother." Phaedra offered, then walked off towards the castle once more. Donovan tried to stop her, but Tobias reached out to block his hand.

"Let her go, Donovan. You are not done with each other. Your time with Typhon and Hope is done for now, but you will meet up again."

Donovan looked utterly defeated. He watched Phaedra walk out of his life, maybe forever. He had a need to protect her. It nagged him as he stood there and watched her leave. "So much loss. I don't know what to do."

"Meet your true family, we will support you."

Phaedra walked right into the castle the same way they left. She found her brother still unconscious from blood loss. She took a dagger from a nearby soldier's body and cut her arm and placed it in his mouth. A few drops escaped in between his lips. His eyes opened and he saw her breasts as they heaved over his body. He smelled her scent, tasted her blood, his senses jolted. He sucked her blood into his mouth then yanked himself upright and threw her over his shoulder. She squeaked in surprise. Typhon tossed her down on the bed with a thud.

"Damnit, Phaedra, how could you just leave me here to wither away or whatever the nine hells happens to blood suckers when they lose blood?"

"*Me*? Do you even know what *you* were doing?"

He looked confused. "No, what?"

"Never mind. Let's get out of here. Donovan's gone with King Rosedale. It was the..."

"Rosedale? Here? What would bring him to Surilla? They're enemies."

"I need more blood, Phae, can you help me?"

"Yes, here." She leaned her head to the side, pulling her long hair away from her nape. She shut her eyes and waited.

"Gods, this is so weird." He sighed and took her into his strong arms. She felt his lips on her neck. As his fangs settled into her soft flesh, he pulled her close. Phaedra felt him grow hard. Her hips were held against his. He lifted his head for a moment and groaned in pleasure and her gaze locked on his face, so animalistic, so otherworldly. Blood dripped on her chest as it heaved. She felt vulnerable. Her stomach filled with butterflies and tickled. His hand cupped her cheek and he looked deeply into her eyes. "Phae, I don't want to lose you too. We have to do this. Let me share my power with you. Please don't be afraid."

She nodded, although she didn't quite understand. He pressed a soft kiss to her forehead. He cut a slit into his bare chest and bled. Phaedra looked at him one last time and put her mouth to his chest and licked the ambrosia he provided.

"Ooooh, it's good." She sounded surprised. He held her arm to his mouth and drank of her at the same time until they were both breathless. "Why am I turned on so much for you, brother?"

"It is the way of this species of vampire. If we...then you would transform into someone like me."

She licked his wound one last time and shivered. "Are you also feeling this?"

He smiled at her naïve question. He stood back and looked down at his bulging manhood. She gasped then looked in his eyes.

"We have to stop. I can barely control myself." She said.

"I know."

"Okay, you have to let go of me."

"I know."

"Typhon."

"Phaedra."

"Damn it."

He pushed her against the wall and pushed her hips up and slid himself into her wetness. When he was fully within her, they both sighed in relief. His hips pounded into hers. It felt like coming home, like...Hope all over again. She eagerly met his thrusts with her own.

Back in the castle main chamber, Cassian showed Hope that her beloveds had abandoned her. That Typhon was obviously in love with his sister, and Donovan left completely.

"Now, my beloved Seelie, take me as your mate and start the family you want, with me and only me." He held out his hand to her.

She looked at his offered hand and dried her tears. She stood before him and took his hand. "I will never love you, Cassian."

"That's okay. No one else will ever have you but me. You will be happy."

"I doubt it."

Cassian grew angry and kissed her hard. "Doubt me, then. I can also make you miserable, Seelie bitch. Choice is yours." He stalked away and left her alone. She collapsed into a heap of tears on the bed.

Typhon and Phaedra were enmeshed in lovemaking when they realized they were up against a tree, not a wall. They stopped the vampiric transformation when Typhon, almost naked, put her behind him and looked around cautiously. The smell of odd flowers and herbs hung musky in the air.

"I have no idea where we are." Typhon said.

"Me either." She whispered.

"You have to be quiet, Phae, let's find our way out of here, find Hope and Donovan and regroup. Something bigger than I thought is going on."

"I love Donovan. I don't know what I will do if I never see him again."

"You will. Our destiny lies together. Somehow, someway, we'll circle back together."

Dedication

♥

Thank you Tony for being my biggest support and rock. I love you. And to Misha my co-pilot! You rock dear! Thank you, Unbound Publishing LLC for giving me a chance. And to those of you who this book is meant for: the readers! Without you, my dreams wouldn't be coming true. To my best friends: Kelly, Donny, Chad, and Jenny. To my son, may you find a love that takes your breath away.

Made in the USA
Middletown, DE
07 May 2024

53961331R00070